I0659561

Haunted Ohio Unearthed

Real Ghost Stories from the Shadows of the Buckeye State
Written and illustrated
by Jannette Quackenbush

ISBN-13: 978-1-940087-75-7

Jannette Quackenbush is an author of over 50 books, folklorist, naturalist, and paranormal researcher. She focuses on ghost stories, folklore, and hiking trails in the Appalachian and southern U.S. Known for her engaging storytelling, she has published many works on local legends and haunted places. Her project, "Dark Journeys with Jannette," features guided hikes where participants explore haunted sites and learn about the region's folklore, connecting them to the rich cultural history and stories of the area. People always ask me, "Do you believe?" And here is how I feel, "Everybody is a skeptic until they experience something out of the norm. Then, all of a sudden, they realize there is more out there to discover, and they become part of this big community of others whose eyes are open to the unknown. And they want to know more, see more, adventure more. Do I believe? Well, I'd certainly rather be racing out to be with the believers, the adventurous ones who get out and explore. You can be among this community too—just get out there!"

The Pale Shade of Dunkinsville
(Adams County)

A Bridge That Never Sleeps

There's a bridge outside Dunkinsville—a rust-bitten span of iron and shadow stretched across the black waters of Brush Creek. For decades, folks said something walked there after dark.

Not walked exactly—glided.

Slid like a sorrow through the cold.

She's seen only at night—when the dark grows heavy, and the world forgets to stir.

Barefoot in the Frost

They say she comes silent, barefoot, the wet surface of pebbles and concrete on the bridge never making a sound beneath her. She's dressed all in black—no shawl, no coat—though the air cuts like a blade in winter. Her long black hair hangs in snarls down her back, whipped by the wind. Her hands are corpse-pale, and one of them is always raised, shielding a face that is somehow even whiter, as if drained dry. You don't see her eyes. You see death.

She does not speak.

She does not pause.

The Man Who Saw Her

Still trembling when he told it, one man said he was crossing the bridge with others one icy night when she passed right by them. Brushed their shoulders. Not a word. Not a sound. Just that shroud of black, that hair twisted in the wind, and a face that looked more like a wax death mask than flesh. He said, "Her hand was so pale it seemed to glow, and it covered her face like she couldn't bear to be seen—not by the living."

But they all saw her. And they remembered.

The Girl Who Left No Footprints

The old folks knew who she was.

They remembered Julia Eichel, a servant girl who vanished one winter when the ground was hard, and the snow lay two inches thick. She'd said goodnight to her employer, a merchant in town. Went to her room.

That was the last time anyone saw her alive.

Come morning, the house was quiet. Julia hadn't stirred. When they checked her room, they found her hat and her shoes neatly placed at the foot of the bed—like she was still asleep. But the bed was empty.

The doors locked.

No signs of struggle.

No tracks in the yard.

Not even a smudge in the snow.

She had simply vanished. Swallowed by the cold. Or by something far older than winter.

What the Bridge Remembers

And now, she walks the bridge.

No one dares call out to her.

No one asks what she wants.

Because if she ever lowers that hand—and shows you her face—you'll understand what it means to be claimed by the dead.

The Headless Coachman of Wickerham's Inn

(Adams County)

There was once a tavern—half-home, half-waystation—set along the twisting wilds of Zane's Trace, a lonely road that sliced through southern Ohio like a scar. Built by pioneer Peter Wickerham near present-day Peebles, it stood along what is now State Route 41. Like many frontier inns, it offered food, drink, and a place to sleep—for those weary or unlucky enough to pass through the dark by stagecoach.

The Wickerham Inn earned a solid name for fifty years: dependable, quiet, proper. But that's only half the story. The rest has been whispered for generations. The rest still stains the floorboards.

It began in the early 1800s.

He Never Left the Room

One bitter evening, a stagecoach driver arrived late. He was road-worn, soaked in cold mud, and itching for ale. He sat by the fire, said little, and drank alone. But before bed, he let slip—carelessly, fatally—that he carried a large sum of money in his coat.

That was the last anyone heard him speak.

Come morning, a worker went to wake the driver.

But the man was gone.

And something else was waiting in the room instead.

The Room of Red

There was blood—so much blood. Splashed up the walls. Dripping from the windowsill. A trail of it soaked into the floorboards, black and sticky. Entrails had been flung like garbage, twisted across the floor. And beside the bed lay a wet outline, the shape of a man, still warm but headless.

The body was missing.

So was the head.

The inn was scrubbed clean. No report was made. No body, no crime. Just whispers. The story, some said, was nothing more than tavern gossip—an ugly rumor born of ale and shadows.

But the floor never forgot.

There was a bloody imprint beside the bed that refused to vanish. It bled through even after scrubbing, repainting, and boarding it over.

The Ghost in the Glass

Years passed. The inn changed hands. The road changed shape—gravel became pavement. But strange things continued.

Travelers saw the figure of a headless man standing at the upstairs window.

Others saw him pacing the grounds at night, hand pressed to where a head should be as if still searching for what had been stolen.

The stain by the bed remained. It pulsed darker in the rain. And then, in 1922, came the truth no one wanted.

The Bones Beneath

During renovations, a construction crew working in the cellar struck something hard. At first, they thought it was rock. But it was bone. A human skeleton curled beneath the dirt like it had been tossed in a hurry. Arms bent backward. Ribs cracked. Jaw slack in eternal horror.

But there was no skull.

The skeleton was pulled out and taken away. But the upstairs room grew colder. The glass in the window cracked as if something had knocked from the inside.

No one stays there now. Not willingly. They say the stain still seeps through the wood. They say the headless man still waits—pacing through the dark— listening for the sound of hoofbeats that will never come.

The Lantern Flame of Lima
(Allen County)

The ground is flat now—grassy sports fields, chain-link fences, and neat rows of aging houses with trimmed hedges and concrete driveways. But beneath them—something older stirs. Before the streets were laid, before the cul-de-sacs curled in like a noose, this patch of land on the outskirts of Lima held a farmstead...and cemeteries. Two of them. Forgotten now. Their stones crumbled. Their names worn to sand. Only overgrown patches of grass hint at what's buried beneath.

But when the cold sets in—something rises.

The Flickering Flame

It begins in the fall and deepens with the winter fog. Along Elizabeth, North Main, and North Union streets, around midnight, a tiny wavering flame begins to drift through the dark. It floats at the height of a man's shoulders. It never hurries.

It moves like a memory.

Witnesses say the flame travels the same route each time, drifting to where an old spring once bubbled up from the earth behind the houses. It pauses there—hesitating—before vanishing. And then, moments later, it returns, retracing its ghostly path.

The Old Man Who Wouldn't Rest

People say there once was a farmer who lived on that land long ago—a crooked old man who walked to the spring each night. In one hand, he carried a dented tin bucket. In the other, a lantern.

He'd light his way across the dirt paths that later became paved roads, set his lantern in the brush, and stoop to fill his bucket with cold spring water. Then he'd pick it up and shuffle back to the farmhouse without a word.

Some say he still takes that walk.

Even in death.

The Night It Followed Them Back

One winter night, just after the first snow dusted the sidewalks, a group of passersby spotted the light and decided to follow it.

One man, who later refused to give his name, told the story in a whisper: "It looked like a little flame—flickering, dancing through the dark. We thought we'd just watch where it went. But as we got closer, something stepped out beside it... like the shadow of a man bent by age. I swear he had no lantern, but his hands were curled up like they were still holding one. You could see every bone in his fingers. His back was hunched like he was bent under years of rot. And he turned to us... not with a face, just a shape. But I felt it. That thing looked at us. And what I felt—was hate. Like the cold wind that hits you when you pass something dead in the road. Bitter. Wet. Foul." They turned back. Fast.

They say the light didn't chase them—but it watched.

When they returned home, none of them could sleep. For nights afterward, the men reported nightmares they couldn't shake—visions of blackened eyes, rotting fields, and skeletal hands reaching up through cellar doors. One man refused to return to the neighborhood altogether.

They looked for footprints in the snow. There were none.

What Walks There Now

Maybe it's just the spirit of a long-dead farmer, condemned to his nightly routine. But others believe it's something older. Something buried where it shouldn't have been. Something that remembers being disturbed.

The cemeteries are gone. The spring is capped.

But the flame still walks.

And if you follow it too far...you might not come back the same.

Celia Rose and the Cottage Cheese Killings
(Allen County)

It was the morning of June 24, 1896—humid and hot, the kind of day where flies stuck to the screen doors and the milk curdled early. David Rose, a miller and farmer living in the wooded heart of Pleasant Valley, burst into the nearby village of Newville in a panic. His wife, Rebecca, was violently ill. She had barely finished her breakfast before she started retching, her body seized by convulsions, her mouth frothing, eyes rolling back.

But David wouldn't make it far. Before the doctor could even gather his supplies, David collapsed on the roadside—gasping, sweating, and vomiting blood. He had to be hauled back home in a horse cart, slumped and howling in pain.

And he wasn't the only one dying.

A House of Slow Deaths

David died on June 30, and the heat in the valley turned heavy with rot. He wasn't the only one dying.

Walter Rose, David's son, followed, writhing in bed until July 4, dying as fireworks echoed through the hills.

And then Rebecca—who had shown signs of recovery—turned pale and stopped breathing July 19. Within ten days, three members of the Rose family were dead. Their bowels burned. Their skin blistered. They had not died easy. And the cause was clear: arsenic.

Specifically, a household poison known as Rough on Rats—an innocent tin kept in the pantry.

Someone had stirred it into the cottage cheese.

The Girl Who Didn't Die

Only Celia Rose, called Ceely, remained. The youngest. The sweetest. The one that was *different.*

She had the mind of a child and the body of a woman, and neighbors knew her odd, staring silences. She followed people. She clung too long. She didn't seem to know where the line between kindness and love began.

Celia had fixated on a neighbor boy.

She wandered to his house daily.

Brought him gifts. Stood in his yard.

His father grew uneasy, and David Rose, kind as he was, finally scolded her.

That was when Celia stopped speaking to her family. And shortly after, she served them cottage cheese for breakfast. And they died.

The Confession and the Trap

She didn't cry when they died. She didn't flinch at the funerals. Some said she seemed... pleased. Or maybe just unmoved, like she hadn't understood what death meant. Or maybe she did.

A local prosecutor set a trap—enlisting Theresa Davis, a former schoolmate, to play confidante. To play traitor. Theresa told Celia she had kept secrets for bad people before, and Celia, eager to feel understood, spoke plainly: "I put Rough on Rats in the cottage cheese. They wouldn't let me be with him."

It took the jury less than an hour.

Life After Life

She was convicted of three murders but spared the gallows—declared criminally insane and sent to Lima State Hospital.

She lived behind locked doors for nearly four decades, wandering its corridors in her slippers, mumbling stories to no one.

She died on March 14, 1934, and was buried beneath a plain white cross.

Just one of 476 identical graves in that old, forgotten asylum cemetery.

But hers is different. Just like her.

The Ghost of Celia Rose

On Celia's grave, someone nailed a warped wooden frame. Inside is her picture. A young woman with downcast eyes staring just past the camera. She is easy to miss. But harder to forget.

Because some say she never left.

Visitors to the cemetery have seen a woman walking between the rows of crosses—stooped, pale, muttering to herself. She carries something unseen in her hands. Her face seems empty until you meet her gaze.

And then she smiles.

Not kindly.

Knowingly.

Some say she doesn't notice you. Others swear she follows them to the gate.

Maybe Celia Rose never truly understood what she'd done. Or maybe she understood just enough.

She only wanted to be with the boy next door.

And the ones who stood in her way?

She killed them. Quietly. Completely. Gone.

Now she walks alone, still searching.

And if she looks your way—don't stand between her and what she wants.

She had her reasons then.

She still does.

The Bone-Thieved Corpse's Lantern
(Ashland County)

Long ago, before Mohican was forested and named, before the trails were cut or the tourists came, a man named Paul Lyons lived out in the wild.

A logging man. A quiet man. He hunted what moved, hauled what paid, and worked his back bloody for what little he had. His wife cooked by lantern light. His boy ran barefoot through the gullies. Then one day—Paul died.

The Crushing

It happened in the timber-cutting season of 1856.

Paul was hauling logs near the falls—two heavy trunks dragging behind a team on wet ground. Something slipped. The chain snapped.

The logs rolled. They didn't just crush him.

They folded him—snapped his spine like a stick of kindling, and left his skull caved in, one eye dangling loose in the dirt. The sound echoed through the gorge, and his son was the one who found what was left of him, twitching.

They buried him on the hill between two waterfalls, where the trees still weep sap, and the mist never lifts. Someone carved a name on a wooden marker and left it there to rot.

The Grave Robber

But Paul Lyons was not left to rest.

Some years after, a doctor—one of those cold-handed ghouls with glass souls and no grace—dug him up in the night. He cracked open the coffin, yanked out the bones, and stripped Paul of his flesh like a butcher dressing meat.

The skeleton was boiled, wired, mounted—used to teach bright-eyed medical students about the structure of man. They didn't know that man had a name. They didn't know that man still walked.

Today, the marker is gone. All that remains is a sunken scar in the earth. A hole that doesn't heal. The kind the dead fall back into again and again.

The Lantern That Shouldn't Burn

But the woods, remember.

And sometimes, the lantern returns.

On damp nights, when the fog clings low, and the air tastes like rust, hikers have seen it—a flicker on the ridge, too far from any trail. It sways like it's carried by a man with a broken neck.

Some say if you follow it, you'll hear the rattle of bones.

Others say you'll see the shadow of a man walking with his arms outstretched—as if he's still looking for the body they took from him.

And if the light turns toward you—if it moves faster—run.

He's still searching for what's rightfully his.

And he does not remember who took it.

She floats at Hereford Station
(Ashland County)

Just south of New London, where Buck Creek winds through the valley, and the trees lean a little too close to the rails, there once stood a rail stop called Hereford Station. It was named—so the story goes—for the Hereford cattle bred by a local man named Knowlton whose land the B&O Railroad cut through in the 1890s.

It wasn't just a platform in the weeds.

There was a depot. A hotel. A restaurant. A coal yard. Cattle pens. A pump house. A water tower.

For a while, it thrived—a brief, beating pulse in the long line of rails heading east and west.

Now, the station is long gone. But the ground still remembers. And so, it's said, does something else.

The Pale Woman Beside the Rails

She was seen during the station's heyday. Always at night. Always alone. Sometimes peering into windows of the homes. Railmen spoke of a woman in a rotting pale dress, soaked from the hem up as if she'd climbed from the creek. She drifted along the trackside, never walking fast, never speaking, her hair dripping across her shoulders, her hands curled like they were gripping something that wasn't there. She would vanish at the curve of the woods. Or be seen again—kneeling by the creek.

Sometimes in the water. Sometimes, in the middle of the rails, staring at nothing. No one knew her name. No one knew where she came from. But the sightings kept on until the station shut down. And even then, some said the tracks themselves held her path like a scar.

What's Left

Today, you'd never know Hereford Station stood there unless you were looking at the old maps. The buildings are gone, but the tracks still run just off State Route 60, and a few houses still stand nearby—quiet, their windows dark after sundown. If you're passing through on a fog-heavy night, and your headlights catch something pale where it shouldn't be—don't stop. And don't look too long. They say she never paid attention to the trains. But she might notice you.

The Night the Bridge Gave Way to the Ghosts
(Ashtabula County)

The snow fell hard that night. Thick, callous, and wet, it blanketed the village of Ashtabula in two feet of white silence. But it wasn't quiet. The wind came screaming down the lake, tearing through eaves and chimneys, gusting at 40 miles per hour like it wanted to rip the town from its foundation. Out on the tracks, the Pacific Express No. 5 pushed through the drifts, groaning westward at a cautious 15 miles per hour.

Just three-tenths of a mile from the depot, the lights of home glinted through the storm. It should've been a short, easy coast to safety. Inside the 11 cars—baggage, sleepers, coaches, the drawing room—families dozed and children squirmed. There were 159 souls aboard. Men in stiff collars. Women clutching satchels. Holiday travelers. An old hog farmer named Clemens. A boy selling newspapers. Effie Neely, eighteen, coming back from Niagara Falls with her sweetheart. Philip Bliss, the hymn writer, returning to Chicago with his wife, Lucy.

What the Eye Missed

The bridge over the Ashtabula River looked sturdy enough. It had held countless times before. But deep in its iron bones, a crack had grown—born years earlier in a hidden air hole, spreading like rot.

The steel was brittle. The joints were tired. And when the weight of the locomotives met the cold steel that night, the structure gave up with a shudder.

The lead engine made it across.

Everything else did not.

Seventy Feet Down

With a roar, the train was swallowed by the dark. The bridge folded inward, rails curling like snakes as cars slammed into one another, then dropped—seventy feet—into the frozen river and the stone bank below.

Some were crushed the moment they fell. Others lay broken in the darkness, screaming for help. Then the lamps broke. The coal stoves split open. And the flames came. The fire tore through the splintered cars in minutes. Wood shrieked as it burned. Skin blistered.

People clawed the snow to escape the heat, but many never made it past the wreckage.

Some were trapped. Some chose to stay—like Philip Bliss, who refused to leave his pinned wife. He perished beside her in the blaze. Rescuers pulled Effie Neely from the fire. Her lover died trying to save others. By dawn, the river steamed with heat and death.

Too Broken to Bury

Ninety-eight people died. Sixty-four more were left shattered. But worse still—forty-eight bodies could not be identified. The heat had taken away their faces. The weight of the wreck crushed them to pulp and bone splinters. What could be gathered was burned, buried in a mass grave, or scraped from the ice and shoveled into boxes.

Buttons. Shoes. Charred rings. A mother's bonnet. That was all some families ever saw again.

They say the stench of scorched flesh lingered in Ashtabula for days—trapped in the riverbanks, soaked into the rail ties.

What the River Remembers

Years passed. Laws changed. Bridges were built better.

But something stayed behind. Walk the edge of the Ashtabula River when the snow falls heavy, and the wind moves wrong, and you might see the shadows rise. Mist, thick as smoke, crawls from the water where the bridge once stood. Some say they take the shape of women holding children. Others are just smears of light, drifting without legs. There are sounds, too—high, shrill cries like steam whistles beneath the ice.

Sometimes it's a name. Sometimes it's just screaming. They float toward the bank. Then vanish. But the ground remembers. And so does the water. The fire is gone. The bridge is gone. But the dead are still moving.

They say if you stand too long by the banks—especially in the dead of winter when the snow hangs in the air like ash, and the water runs black—you'll see shapes walking the river. Not drifting. Walking.

Figures stagger up from the place where the train fell. Some crawl with limbs twisted the wrong way. Some have no heads. Some still clutch what's left of a child, a satchel, a hymnbook scorched to nothing. Their feet never touch the snow. Their mouths hang open, gasping for screams that never reach the surface.

Sometimes, they wander into the trees. Sometimes, they just pace the bank, back and forth, like they're looking for something they lost in the water. And sometimes—if the wind dies and you listen very close—you'll hear it. Not the river. Not the wind. *The bridge.*

It starts low, like a groan deep underground. Then a screech—steel giving way. Screams. The crunch of timbers snapping. The roar of a thousand tons falling.

It all comes back. Every shriek. Every crack. Every death. Like the night is tearing open again.

And if you don't turn away if you just stand there and listen—you'll feel it underneath you. The rails buckling. The ground falling out. And a hundred dead hands reaching up from below.

The bridge falls.

And this time, it takes you with it.

The Shadow That Follows the Children
(Ashtabula County)

In the winter-bitten hills east of Ashtabula, the McAdams family worked a modest patch of land—twelve souls beneath one timber roof, a house groaning under the weight of its own silence.

Their eldest, Jeanette, was a strange girl, even as a child. Dark-haired, with eyes like polished coal and cheeks the color of bruised roses, she could have been lovely—if only she'd been like the others.

She wasn't.

She dressed in men's trousers, unheard of at this time.

She wandered into the woods after sundown.

She disappeared for days and returned soaked to the skin, saying nothing. No one asked where she went. Not after the second time her fingers came back stained black. Eventually, she left for Cleveland. The family didn't speak of her often, though she still returned now and then, each visit more unsettling than the last.

That's when the children began to die.

The Sickness That Came with Her

The first was Julia, age thirteen. A clever girl with bright eyes, preparing to leave for school. The night her sister arrived unannounced, Julia turned pale. By morning, her mouth was wet with foam, and she was dead in her bed.

Then came Arthur, only eight years old.

He'd eaten an apple and sipped cider near the hearth. Within the hour, his body convulsed so violently that he cracked his own teeth. His limbs bent backward, and he died screaming for his mother.

Abigail, twenty-one, was next. She'd taken a single piece of candy from Jeanette's coat pocket. They found her curled in the corner of her room with black vomit on her chest.

Then Walter, fourteen, who fell like a felled ox in the yard, howling in agony.

And Luther, twelve, who died clutching his stomach in the field, eyes turned to glass.

Every time—Jeanette had just returned.

Every time—she was there when they died.

No one said a word.

Not aloud.

Then Rebecca, the mother, took sick. Jeanette claimed she would nurse her. Said she had medicine. A white powder. Something the doctor gave.

But the doctor hadn't prescribed anything.

And by sunrise, Rebecca McAdams was cold in the bed.

That was the last time anyone saw Jeanette in town.

The Cemetery That Breathes

Years passed. The farmhouse fell in. The father died alone.

But Edgewood Cemetery—the little plot where the McAdams children were buried—began to whisper.

Grave diggers wouldn't stay past dark.

They claimed they saw shadows, tiny ones, hovering just above the grass-covered graves like smoke on water. Small, flickering forms—no bigger than a child—floating between the stones. But the worst came later.

Visitors sometimes saw another shape rise behind the others. Tall. Cloaked in black that shimmered like wet bark. Its mouth open, but no sound came out. It moved with its head tilted—as if listening. As if counting.

Sometimes, the little shadows would scatter.

Sometimes, they'd vanish altogether.

And the tall one would follow, dragging something behind her—something that dripped.

Locals began to say the name again: *Jeanette.*

What She's Still Looking For

They say she poisoned them. Every one of them.

No one knows why.

Some believe she made a deal.

Some say she simply hated the light in her siblings' eyes.

But they all agree on this—she never left Edgewood Cemetery.

And if you go there now—if you walk among those graves after dark—you might see her.

Not all at once. Just the shape of her coat.

The glint of her eyes.

Her face was too pale. Her hands, too, still.

And if she does see you—if she mistakes you for one of the ones she lost—she'll follow.

She'll follow you home.

And she'll keep following until you're with her, too.

The Hollow That Calls Them Back

(Athens County)

The storm cracked the sky like a bone. Wind screamed through the hollows. Trees thrashed and bent, and from somewhere high above the hills, a plane engine roared through the chaos.

Inside a weather-worn two-story house—about five miles outside of Nelsonville—a couple and their three children stood still in the kitchen, staring out the window above the sink. They could hear it. A plane.

Circling. Dipping in and out of the thunder.

Only the grandfather stayed seated.

Slumped in a threadbare recliner, hands laced across his belly, staring at the blank wall.

The plane's roar came low, then vanished.

Then came again.

Then silence.

The children held their breath.

Lightning lit up the sky, and the parents pressed their faces to the window, hoping for a glimpse. Instead, the hills lit up with a flash—and a muffled, bone-deep explosion rattled the walls.

A scream burst from the kids. Then came nothing but wind and rain again, as if the earth had swallowed the sound whole.

The parents ran. They tore through the living room, grabbing coats and car keys, ready to risk the flooded backroads to reach the police. No phone. No sirens. Just the storm. But before they could reach the door, the grandfather stirred.

"You don't need to go out there in that storm," he said, voice low and hollow.

The woman froze. "What do you mean we don't need to? That plane just crashed—someone could still be alive out there!"

The old man shook his head.

His eyes were too dark, too calm.

"They're not alive," he said. "They've been dead thirty years."

The Crash That Didn't Stay Dead

On May 17th, 1941, a twin-engine military plane—fighting gale-force winds and drowning in thick rain—slammed into a hillside outside Nelsonville.

The pilot could not find the field.

Instead, the plane tore through three hundred feet of trees, ripping the ground open, shearing off bark, burying metal deep in the clay. The explosion was so loud it shook windowpanes across the valley. Bodies were burned beyond recognition.

All five men aboard were killed.

The wreckage was swallowed by the hollow.

The townspeople, police, and military searched that night by flashlight and lightning. They found pieces. A boot. A belt buckle fused to a thigh bone. A face with no jaw. The rest had been scattered. Some say birds got to them before the men did.

Some say the hollow took what was left and never gave it back.

The Shadow in the Trees

The next morning, the couple drove to where they'd heard the explosion. The roads were washed in mud. A few trees still bore the old scars—bark twisted in strange, unnatural patterns.

And up along the hillside, they found the gouges.

Faint. Overgrown. But still there.

Like the earth had tried to forget—but couldn't quite.

Then they saw it.

A single bent shape near the tree line. Black. Still.

A strange lean, like it was frozen in mid-step.

At first, they thought it was a shadow. But it didn't move with the trees. It didn't sway. It stayed perfectly still, crooked at the neck. When they stepped toward it— it vanished.

They turned back immediately.

But before they left, the grandfather had one last thing to say. "You stay away from that place," he warned, voice like a nail sliding across old wood. "Nothing good ever came out of that hollow." He looked out the window then, eyes cloudy like something looking through him. "It calls things in. And it don't let 'em out. Planes. People. Doesn't matter. There's things up there you don't want to know about."

They never asked what those things were.

But now—they understand.

Because when the thunder drags its belly across the hills, the plane comes back.

Not whole. Not right. Just the sound of it, gnawing through the storm.

And every time it circles, it's still searching—for bodies already buried. For voices that haven't spoken in decades.

But sometimes...it finds something else.

And when it does—it doesn't let go.

The Weeping Angel of West State Street in Athens

(Athens County)

In Athens, there's a second city.

It doesn't have lights. It doesn't make noise.

It is the land that sheltered the dead.

West State Street Cemetery holds the bones of the first who came—settlers who fought back the woods. They lived, died, and were buried here—laid to rest in the land they tried to tame.

When they perished, they were laid beneath crooked stones and low hills, swallowed slowly by moss and time.

Watching over them is a statue the town calls the Weeping Angel. Cut from white Italian marble, she stands atop a pedestal with hands resting on a book. Erected by Athens High School in 1924, she was meant to mark the nameless graves beneath her feet—those buried without records since 1804.

But over the years, the stories changed.

She stopped being just a monument.

She became something else.

Three Photos

I was told this by a man who passed through Athens in 2004:

"That statue... I took three pictures of her.

First one, her eyes were closed.

Second one—eyes still closed.

Third one? Her eyes were open.

I didn't move. The statue didn't move. But they were open. Still messes me up, because that thing's made of cement."

He said some kids were walking past the cemetery after school that day. One boy in particular—quiet, like he'd seen too much for his age—was asked:

"Aren't you scared walking through here?"

The boy didn't blink. He just said: "I live in the house right there. And if you want to see something...wait 'til it's raining and there's a full moon. That's when you can see her wings flap."

Not Mourning—Guarding

Locals call her the Weeping Angel, but it's not grief that holds her there.

It is purpose.

She watches over the nameless dead. Not gently. Not sweetly. *Fiercely.*

When the weather turns violent, and the moon pushes through the storm clouds, she's said to move. Her wings twitch. Her eyes follow you.

She doesn't protect you from the dead.

She protects them—from being disturbed. From being forgotten. From being unburied.

And if you walk through West State Street Cemetery on the wrong night, with the wrong intention—you might see her move.

Not just feel it.

See it.

Her head turns just enough to follow you.

Her wings twitch—like they remember how to lift.

And her eyes, carved from blank stone, aren't as closed as they were when you walked in.

People say they've seen it.

Some in photographs.

Some in person.

And all of them say the same thing:

It's not the movement that haunts you.

It's that you know she wanted you to see it.

Bloody Bridge
(Auglaize County)

In the 1850s, the Miami and Erie Canal was a slit in the earth—a long, winding wound from Toledo to Cincinnati. Mules walked the towpath, dragging packet boats through water black with silt and secrets.

In the murky stretch between Spencerville and St. Marys, two boats passed each other often—the Daisy and the Minnie Warren—and with them, two souls bound for tragedy.

Jack Billings worked the Daisy.

Jack was a wide-shouldered man, callused hands, slow smile—he spoke softly to his mule and sang to the towpath. Minnie, daughter of the Minnie Warren's captain, cooked aboard her father's boat and kept to herself until she met Jack.

The first time their boats passed, she tossed him a biscuit and dared him to say the Daisy was faster. He called back that hers was so slow it made the turtles laugh. That's how it started—flirting over dark water.

It didn't take long before they fell deeply in love.

Hard.

Jack counted the days between sightings. Minnie listened for the clip of hooves on packed dirt, wondering if it might be his.

But someone else watched them, too.

William Jones was the mule driver for the Minnie Warren. Sour, quiet, and mean. He loved Minnie with a bitterness that curdled everything it touched. But he was invisible to her. She only had eyes for Jack.

So William waited. And seethed.

And sharpened.

Fall. 1854.

The three of them had attended a dance near the canal—lamplight flickering, music like fiddlebones in the dark. Minnie and Jack had walked home laughing, hand in hand, their path winding along the canal's edge. They stopped at a small wooden bridge just before midnight, where the fog clung to the planks like a dying breath.

That's when William struck.

The ax came from the shadows—quick, brutal, silent. It cleaved through Jack's neck with a sound like splitting green wood. His body dropped, and blood sprayed across the planks.

Minnie screamed once.

Then, she fell backward into the canal. Some say William shoved her. Some say she jumped. Others whisper that when Jack's heart stopped, hers simply unraveled.

Either way—

She didn't rise.

The Water Remembers

They found them the next morning.

Jack's head nearly off, face frozen in surprise.

Minnie's body bobbed just beneath the bridge, skirts tangled in the reeds, hair fanned like riverweed. They pulled her from the canal and laid her beside him. The blood had soaked the wood. It never truly washed away.

For nearly forty years, no storm, no sun, no scraping could remove the stain. The locals called it Bloody Bridge. And they still do.

Those who traveled to the bridge late at night and leaned over the edge would see Minnie floating below, her pale face staring back. Eyes closed as if sleeping. Mouth moving soundlessly as she lay in the water.

Some say she's trying to scream.

Others say she's still calling Jack.

Phantom of Dughill Bridge
(Auglaize County)

Ten miles from Lima, just off Ohio 198, where it hooks into Dughill Road, there's a sloping scar of land gouged deep by the Auglaize River. The hill rises steep and choked with trees, the kind of woods that hum with whispered warnings. Long ago, the hill was gutted, and the river spanned by a wooden bridge—first a rickety pass of rotting planks, then a stronger span with iron. The men who built it named it Dughill Bridge, for the earth they hacked away. But something else claimed it.

The Death of Gaskill

In the autumn of 1860, a man named Gaskill rose early to hunt. He brought his boy along and led him toward the banks near the bridge, where wild game was known to gather at a salt lick. The elder Gaskill was practiced and precise—he'd climb a low tree to watch, and when the time came, his son would pass the rifle up to him.

But a limb caught the hammer. The weapon fired as the boy lifted it. The shot hit Gaskill under the jaw and tore through the base of his skull. They say he tumbled from the branches without a sound, hitting the dirt in a crumpled heap. His son found no breath in him.

Just blood and bone. The earth drank deep.

The Bridge Changed After That

They buried Gaskill in Cridersville, but the woods didn't let him go. Not all of him.

Within weeks, people crossing the bridge began to report the same thing—a sound like hooves pounding just behind them, growing louder and closer until it felt like something was about to trample them down.

Some turned and saw nothing. Others... saw him.

A man with half a face, blood still wet on his shirt, teeth missing, eyes gone white with death. He'd come out of the woods at full tilt, mouth gaping, voice twisted into a scream that didn't sound human. He'd chase wagons across the bridge, slap at the backs of horses with hands that didn't always connect—just passed through like smoke. Riders felt breath on their necks.

Cold fingers on their spines. He howled. Every. Night.

Gaskill Returned

By 1875, locals refused to cross Dughill Bridge after sundown. Too many had come back pale, stammering, and with wild eyes. Some said if you walked across alone, he'd leap from the tree where he died—his bloody mouth open wide, jaw swinging loosely by a hinge of muscle, screaming straight into your face. The bridge is gone now—replaced by steel and concrete crossing on Ohio 198 nearby, dull and forgettable, spanning the state route with no memory of what came before. But the old folks still talk—quietly—of stories passed down around kitchen tables and porches, tales their mamas and dads whispered when they passed that place by wagon or on foot, never slowing, never looking too long.

They remember the spot where Gaskill fell. Where the blood pooled thickly. Where his body was dragged away for burial—but something of him never left.

They say the ground keeps what ends in blood.

On moonlit nights, those who stray near the old road report a strange rustling just out of reach—too heavy for leaves, too deliberate for wind. A few have seen him: a tall, gaunt man clawing his way up a tree that isn't there, reaching for a branch that vanished long ago.

Then—he's gone. Just gone. But the scream stays. It tears through the woods with no warning—raw, cracking, filled with something worse than pain. No birds answer. No wind moves. Even the river holds its breath. It doesn't echo. It just sits there. Like a splinter lodged deep in the flesh of the land—working its way toward the bone.

IT Lingers in Egypt Valley
(Belmont County)

Something peculiar lurks in a wild pocket of overgrown scrub meadows mixed with deep, young woodland in Belmont County, Ohio. It is just off Interstate 70, and those who pass along the highway usually sense that there is more to the land than meets the eye. It has an uninviting appearance in certain areas, and justly so.

The once-rich land was stripped clean by seventy years of surface mining.

It left it a bleak and barren wasteland, inhospitable and desolate, with its terrain so deeply gashed and gouged that it is unidentifiable from the once-tidy rolling hillsides of yesteryear.

Not so long in the past, and when there was little more left to steal from the earth, the Ohio Division of Wildlife bought up the dying property, revived the land, and allowed it to heal and grow back to its wild self again. But not all the earth appeared to grasp this fresh start. Those with a keen perception take note, in a particular section, that something had changed, shifted, altered during its plundered past.

It was as if, when peeling back the flesh of the terrain, then gouging out the soul of the land, something wicked was freed from the bowels of the earth.

Something long buried.

Something that should never return.

Something so dreadfully evil, it still walks as if the land beneath its feet is still quite dead.

The Murder of Louiza Fox January 21, 1869

Egypt Valley was once a quiet patchwork of farmland and forest. In the 1820s, a tiny settlement called Egypt grew around Stillwater Creek. A few homes. A schoolhouse. A Methodist church.

And a gristmill where farmers talked over grain and gossip.

In January 1869, something happened there so monstrous it rooted itself in the earth.

Louiza Fox, thirteen years old, was working, like many girls did then, helping in the house of a coal mine owner—Alex Hunter, in Sewellsville. She swept floors, laundered linens, and kept her hands busy before marriage.

She was no older than a sapling.

Thomas Carr was twenty-two.

A miner. A drunk. A braggart with wild stories and a temper full of broken glass. He followed Louiza home too many times. Told her father he was "just watching over her." Then, he asked her to marry him. When she said no, he asked again. And again.

She always said no.

Carr persisted, even after her father confronted him. He grew erratic. Possessive. Dangerous. On January 21st, he followed Louiza again—stalking her at the Hunter house, whispering to her in the corners, lurking near the doors. Her employer tried to keep her safe, but Louiza insisted on leaving with her six-year-old brother, Willy, who had come to walk her home.

Home was close.

Carr was closer.

Near the chestnut trees by the ditch, he stepped from the shadows and asked her again.

When she refused—he cut her throat.

Dragged her body off the path. Left her in the snow with her little brother screaming beside her. Her father found her minutes later, face down in a red melt. Her body torn, her voice forever silenced.

Carr was caught. Hanged. Buried in an unmarked grave in St. Clairsville. Before the rope snapped, he confessed to killing fourteen others. Lies, most of them.

But one stuck.

The Tunnel and the Thing Beneath

Carr admitted to helping kill a man—Alois Ulrich, a German immigrant. With a second killer, Joseph Eisele, he bludgeoned Ulrich's head in the Wheeling Tunnel with a stone, then dragged the ruined corpse into a culvert like trash.

And after that, people started to see things.

Ulrich's ghost began to appear. Not on the floor, but on the ceiling. Swathed in green slime oozing from cemetery runoff and his own putrid skin. One hand pointed at a ruined temple, cracked and bleeding; the other hung limp with half-severed fingers. His mouth did not move.

But still, it spoke. "Let the dead rest."

But the Dead Do Not Rest

The dead don't stay laid. At least the ones that Carr murdered. Years later, when the coal company arrived with its machines in Egypt Valley—its monster, called GEM, the Giant Earth Mover—they erased entire towns. Farmsteads. Barns. Her home. Her grandparent's house. The church Louiza once rode past. The ditch where she died.

But they dug too deep.

Far too deep.

They unearthed something old. Something buried so long ago it forgot its own name. But not its hunger.

It lingers now—not a ghost, but the thing that feeds on ghosts. A thing that savors the scream before the throat opens. It watches the marker placed for Louiza near the spot where her blood froze in the weeds. It waits in the trees where no birds sit. It moves along the ditch.

And it pauses—like it is tasting.

That January evening, to it, was sweet. The struggle. The final pulse. The gruesome, ghastly moment Carr took joy in his deed. Or may have been preparing for it in the days leading up to the murder.

That's what woke it.

That's what keeps it here.

They say if you walk the old roads at dusk, something watches from the trees.

Not a ghost.

Not a man.

Something else.

You might glimpse it—drifting pale just beyond the reach of headlights, where the woods hold their breath. It never runs.

It follows.

Sometimes, it waits in the ditch, crouched low in the place where she died, the earth remembering the shape of her fall. Tasting it. Touching it. Living it. Savoring it.

And sometimes—it steps onto the road.

And chooses the one who won't leave.

The one who looked too long. The one it can take back underground.

Because some things don't just haunt. They hunt.

The White Dog of Bigley Trough
(Belmont County)

There is a place between Flushing and Morristown where the trees grow too close, and the wind forgets to move. Since the late 1700s, settlers followed a rutted path through this stretch of wilderness, drawn westward by hope and hunger.

It was here, nestled in the shoulder of the hills, that a spring once trickled from the rocks—cold, clear, and sweet.

In 1804, a trough was hollowed from a felled log and set beneath the water's flow. It came to be known as Bigley Watering Trough. Teams of oxen drank from it. Children cupped their hands to the stream. It was a place of brief relief—then travel resumed.

But the land never stayed clean for long.

Not far from the trough, beyond the shimmer of the stream, men began to disappear. Wagons were found ransacked. Sometimes, only bones remained. Travelers began to speak of shadowy figures who lingered too long in the trees—men who never drank, only watched.

It became known as a place where good people vanished.

A Stranger at the Fire

One autumn evening, as the leaves burned gold and red on the branches, a family came to rest at the watering place. A man, his wife, and their nine-year-old daughter. They unyoked their weary oxen. The sun dipped behind the trees. Smoke from their fire curled up into a sky full of stars.

It should have been a peaceful night.

It was not.

As dusk slipped into the moonlight, a stranger approached on a tall, black horse—its saddle gleamed, its reins stitched with silver. The man upon it was clean, too clean for the trail, his voice smooth and manner soft. He asked to share their fire, saying he was bound for the Ohio River.

The father hesitated.

But hospitality outweighed instinct.

He agreed.

Only the child's dog—a great white thing, half-wolf by the look of it—seemed to sense what the family could not. It growled low. Never looked away from the stranger. Never blinked.

That night, the stars wheeled overhead.

The fire sank low.

And silence pressed in like a weight.

What They Found

At dawn, a hunting party passed near the trail and found the little girl wandering among the trees, barefoot, face smeared with ash and tears. The white dog walked at her side, stiff-legged and silent, like a sentinel. The child said nothing at first—only pointed with a trembling hand.

The hunters followed her back to camp.

There, they found the bodies.

The mother and father had been butchered in their sleep. Their throats opened clean and wide. The fire had gone out hours ago, and the ground was soaked through with blood. A knife lay nearby, dark to the hilt.

When they asked the girl what she remembered, she could only whisper: "He rode away in the moonlight."

She never said where they were bound. Never spoke of her home. The grief took her within weeks. Her body was buried near the settlers who had taken her in.

The white dog was found curled against her grave the next morning, stiff with death, eyes wide open.

What Walks There Now

The land has changed. Wagons no longer creak along the trail, and no one stops at a trough long lost to rot and overgrowth.

But the place they once called the Bigley Watering Trough is no place for lingering.

At midnight, beneath a cold, full moon, people still report strange sounds in the fields—soft padding through brittle grass, a low, rattling growl, a child's cry swallowed too quickly.

Sometimes, if the sky is clear and the wind still, passersby glimpse a pale figure near where the spring once ran:

A little girl. Cowering just beyond the reach of light.

A white dog, tense at her side.

She never speaks. She only watches.

And then she fades.

But something else grows from the dark hollow where she stood. Something that remembers what was done.

It rises slow, crooked, wrong—a towering shadow born from the blood left behind.

It has no eyes.

But it sees.

It has no voice.

But it hungers.

And it waits— right where the water once ran sweet.

Haunting at Lady Bend Hill
(Belmont County)

Before it was called the National Road—and long before I-70 gutted the hill with concrete and steel—the trail west was known as Zane Trace. It crept across Ohio in ruts and mud, worn by settlers and stagecoaches, their wheels carving scars through forest and field. Just outside Morristown, it dipped sharply into a tangled hollow. The bend at the bottom was sudden and steep— wagon-wrecking, bone-breaking. Many didn't make it through. Even back then, they called it cursed.

The Woman Who Rode In

One spring evening, just as dusk reached the treetops, a lone rider appeared at the door of a small roadside tavern. She was young, composed, and striking in fine riding clothes—a fitted habit, tall boots, gloves without wear. Her dark horse stood silent outside, steam rising from its flanks.

When she entered, the room fell silent.

Voices trailed off. Pipes lowered. Cards held mid-hand.

She removed her gloves, lifted her veil, and politely asked for directions west.

The men in the tavern exchanged looks. Most figured she was a rich girl on the run—fleeing a father's fury to meet some poor lover down the line.

A few guessed darker things: an officer's widow, maybe. Or a wife running not *to* someone, but *from* something.

Whatever the truth, no one asked her name.

And she didn't offer it. But no one asked. And she offered nothing.

After a moment, she turned, stepped back into the night, and closed the door behind her. She was never seen alive again.

Blood on the Trace

At dawn, travelers found her horse grazing by the roadside, still saddled, reins dragging. It snorted once but did not bolt. Not far from it, a riding hat lay in the dirt. Her veil—ripped and stiff with blood—fluttered in the grass.

They searched the woods. Found crushed brush. A tangle of snapped branches. A handprint in the mud.

But no body was discovered.

An old farmer in a shack up the ridge said he heard something just after dark—two sharp cries and a scream that twisted off mid-breath. He said it wasn't a person. Not quite. Sounded more like something split open.

He thought it was an animal fight.

So he stayed inside.

What Was Left

Rumors rose like smoke.

Some said she was followed—cut down for her money, dragged into the woods, buried under leaves.

Others swore her horse had thrown her at the bend, her body lost to the ravine. Wild dogs, perhaps, had done the rest.

But searchers found other things: A silver pin buried in blood-soaked moss. A torn boot with bone still inside. A trail that went halfway down the hill—and stopped. There were no returning footprints. Only drag marks.

And something deeper—clawing upward.

What Walks There Now

The stagecoaches are gone. The wagons no longer creak along the path. But the hill remains.

And some nights, beneath a cold spring moon, travelers hear it—hooves striking just once, a woman's cry cut short, and something heavier moving behind.

Some say they've seen her: A woman in white.

Riding fast toward the curve. A white veil fluttering.

Blood shining at her collar.

She never speaks.

She only stares.

No one knows what secrets she held— or who tore them from her.

She vanishes where the ground drank her blood, and the soil turned black beneath it. And still, she rides.

Night after night.

Her death is a riddle, and those who see her are always wondering, haunted by the woman who rides the place now called Lady Bend Hill.

Calico Lady of Old Lafferty Road
(Brown County)

There are many names for a group of cats: a dout, a clutter, a glaring. If they're feral, they're called a destruction. But the one that sticks—the one that clings to the ribs like old milk—is clowder. From the Middle English clodder, meaning to clot, to coagulate. A clotted mass. And on old Lafferty Road, there once was just that:

A clowder of cats. And the thing that fed them.

At the far bend of a rutted dirt road, along the banks of Lafferty Run, stood a sagging, two-story house with warped shutters and a porch that tilted like it had lost the will to stand. That's where the old woman lived. No family left—just cats. A hundred of them, it seemed. Some say they were strays. Others say they came from her.

She treated them like her children. Named each one. Fed them from a rusted tin bucket she clutched in her bony hand, always banging it with an old spoon as she hobbled through the yard, calling them to supper like a dinner bell rung in hell.

When anyone passed—on horseback, in a truck, or later, in rusted-out Fords—she'd explode from the house in a frenzy, her shin-length calico dress flapping like a banner of war. She'd scream at the top of her lungs, warning folks to slow down before they killed one of her "babies." And always—always—the cats would swarm behind her, hissing and yowling like they were chasing the devil out of town.

She'd run right after the cars, shaking her bucket, spoon clanging like a cowbell in a tornado. It was said she'd lost two fingers on her feeding hand. Not to age or accident. But to her children. They'd gotten too hungry one day, and something got mistaken for a chicken bone.

Then, one day, the old woman went silent.

No shouting. No bucket. No screaming cats.

Weeks passed. Eventually, someone went to the house. It was quiet. Too quiet.

They found her there.

Or what was left of her.

Mostly bone, picked clean, sprawled in the center of the kitchen. The cats had eaten her. Not out of hatred— no, out of habit. Out of hunger. And they didn't stop when they got to the skin. What was left was... pulp. A clotted mass of gray fur, dried gore, skin scraps, and cat waste.

The tin bucket was still clutched in her three-fingered hand.

Several desiccated cat carcasses surrounded her like little mummified mourners.

But That Wasn't the End

After the house began to rot, the stories began.

They said you could still see her on moonlit nights. Hobbling out of the collapsing porch, swarmed by ghostly cats. Her empty eye sockets turned toward the road. The bucket still in hand. Her voice rising up from the hollow, somewhere between a wail and a yowl.

By the 1970s, it became a dare:

Take the winding trail of Chicken Hollow.

Stop at the ruins.

Call for her.

"Calico Lady!"

Sometimes, nothing happened.

Sometimes, cats would appear—just watching.

And sometimes… she came.

A pale, stooped figure in multicolored rags.

Dragging her bucket. Three fingers. No smile. And she ran. Straight at the living. Fast. Raging.

Even if she wasn't a ghost—whatever she was, she meant business. More than one teenager wet themselves and never admitted it. Some said they heard her laugh like a cracked music box.

What's Left Now

The house is gone, eaten by time and ivy. All that remains is a sagging stone foundation, broken chimney bricks, and creek rocks the color of old teeth. The road itself is barely a trail now—choked in weeds, blocked by fallen trees, and fenced off by property lines with "No Trespassing" signs riddled with birdshot.

But the Calico Lady never needed a house.

She needed a place.

And a reason.

Some say she still wanders the edge of the field, just where the trees thicken and the creek whispers where the old foundation stones still lay.

You'll hear the clanging of metal.

The cry of a single cat.

The thump of three fingers against a rusted pail.

And if you hear her call—don't answer.

She fed her children once. But they are hungry again.

Chain-Dragged Dead of Ghost Hollow
(Brown County)

It wasn't the first time the hounds were heard in the hollow between Ripley and Aberdeen.

And it won't be the last.

In the wooded folds near Eagle Creek—where the land warps into steep ravines and the road forgets its own name—folks had whispered for years of the things seen in the dark. Pale figures flickering through the trees.

Dogs that bayed long past death. Groans that came from nowhere. People started calling it Ghost Hollow, though most said it with a nervous laugh and eyes that didn't quite meet yours.

But on the last day of January in 1895, two men walked into that hollow and came out rattled. Changed.

And not everyone believed they left the dead behind.

Two Good Men and One Terrible Night

Thirty-six-year-old Alexander Griffith and fifty-nine-year-old Ephraim "Tip" Martin were respected names in Brown County—God-fearing farmers and trusted neighbors. Griffith had once served as a county commissioner; Tip Martin's handshake alone could settle a land dispute. These weren't drunkards or gossipmongers. They were solid men, and when they talked, people listened.

That is until the night they saw something they shouldn't have.

And told it.

They were walking back from Ripley, six miles into frozen hills and howling dark. The roads were rutted and cruel that time of year, lined with ice-hardened brush and hollows that swallowed light whole. Scarves pulled high, heads down, they trudged toward home, their boots crunching over frost-slick stone.

Then came the sound.

A low, shuddering groan—like something being squeezed out of the earth.

They stopped. Looked. Waited.

Nothing. Just the skeletal trees clacking in the wind.

Then—chain.

The Thing That Ran

Something moved on the slope to their right. Fast. Lurching.

A man.

Or what had once been one.

He came careening down the hill, arms flailing, the clatter of heavy chain dragging behind him. His face— what little they saw—was slick with shadow. His jaw hung open as if he were mid-scream, but no sound came from his mouth. Only the grinding groan of metal links scraping rock.

And then—he was gone.

Swallowed by the night.

Seconds later, the woods came alive again.

Howling.

A pack of foxhounds burst through the brush behind him—yowling, snarling, foam-flecked. Their eyes were too wide. Their shapes too lean. They gave chase through the trees, trailing the sound of dragging chain.

Then—silence. Not even the wind.

The Story That Should Have Stayed Buried

Griffith and Martin told what they saw. The Ripley Gazette ran it under Two Men, One Ghost. Folks in Hillsboro laughed. Others didn't.

Because there was an old story tied to that ravine.

Years earlier, during a fox hunt, a surly man named Joe Woods had brought ten of his best hounds to the holler.

He wasn't well-liked—mean drunk, quick with his fists. But he wanted in on the hunt. The other men refused.

Tempers flared. A brawl broke out.

The foxes got away.

Someone snapped.

The hunters tied Woods to a stump with iron chains. Left him there.

To freeze.

 To rot.

His hounds stayed by his side, wailing for days.

Until they stopped.

No one saw Joe Woods—or his dogs—again.

Not alive, anyway.

Now, When the Wind Turns

Today, they call it Ghost Hollow like it's folklore.

 But some still won't walk that stretch after sundown.

They say if you're quiet, you'll hear the chains first.

 Then, the breathless, wheezing run of something not quite human.

Then the hounds.

They don't bark.

They scream.

And if you see them—don't run.

They remember what their master suffered.

They remember being left behind.

And they're always hungry.

The Oxford Light
(Butler County)

A Lonely Stretch of Road

Long before the pavement was laid and the college crowds filled the town, Oxford-Milford Road was a dark, rutted trail that twisted through woods and farmland. At night, it ran black and silent, flanked by corn stubble, old fence posts, and gnarled trees that clawed the moonlight.

And somewhere along that road—between Oxford proper and the old township line—a light began to appear.

The Lantern That Shouldn't Be

The stories began in the early 1930s, although some old-timers claimed their fathers had seen it before the Great War. Always the same: a single white light, bobbing gently as if held in a walking hand, drifting down the center of the road. It made no sound. It cast no shadow. And when approached, it either vanished suddenly or moved just out of reach.

Some swore it hovered six feet above the ground. Others said it flickered like a lantern caught in a wind that no one could feel.

"It passed right in front of the buggy," one man said in 1934. "Didn't blink. It didn't slow. Just kept on like a man headed for his grave."

The Forgotten Death

The older version of the tale—told only in hush among farm families—tied the light to a man who died in winter, trying to fetch help. His child had taken ill. His wife was sobbing in the doorway. He lit a lantern and stepped into the cold, swearing to reach the neighbor's place two miles down. He never made it.

They found him the next morning, stiff in a ditch, one hand frozen tight around the empty handle. His lantern had shattered—glass shards scattered like teeth in the snow. Whether it was a heart attack or the cold that took him, no one knew. But from that winter on, his light returned. Some believed it was his soul, still searching the road for a doctor who never came. Others said it was a death omen—if the light paused in front of you, someone in your family would die.

And some, mostly children, believed if you followed it far enough into the dark, it would lead you into the trees—and you wouldn't come back.

A Lantern Without a Hand

Through the decades, the story warped.

By the 1950s, teenagers were chasing the light with flashlights and bravado. By the '60s, the ghost had traded his lantern for a motorcycle, and the farmer became a dead college boy from Miami University.

But the real light—the one from the 1930s—still walks, they say. It doesn't roar or rev or scream. It just glides. Smooth and slow.

And if you ever see it standing still in the road—bathed in that cold, flickering light—don't run. It won't matter.

By then, it's already chosen you.

You'll either follow it into the dark and vanish like the rest...or it'll come back with you—quiet, patient, and cruel. And it will take its time.

Angry Ghosts of the West Chester Graveyard

(Butler County)

Based on reports published in the Cincinnati Enquirer, October 21, 1894

Long before the highways, the strip malls, the golf courses, and the gated subdivisions, the land near Tecumseh Creek was quiet. Dense trees lined the stream. A slight rise marked with stone and brush was left untouched. Locals knew not to disturb it—not out of law, but instinct, empathy, and respect.

Before It Was Violated by Greed

It was a graveyard. A sacred place.

In the fall of 1894, that changed.

George Washington Swearingen, too old to work the family land near what's now Liberty Way, leased his farm to a tenant. The man plowed the soil without knowing what lay beneath it. Soon after, he began to hear voices—unfamiliar, murmuring, rising with the dusk wind. Then came the sightings.

The Dead Began to Return

Jacob Hoover, a nearby resident, described what he saw: an old white man standing in a field, surrounded by figures dressed like Miami Indians, their arms raised in agitation, their mouths moving in silence. Behind them, the field glowed faintly red as if lit from underground.

One night, the old white figure turned and began walking toward the farmhand. Not drifting—walking with purpose. The tenant fled. His fear shook the towns around him.

Word spread fast. By week's end, people came from Maud and Chester Station to see for themselves. And they saw spectral reenactments in the field. Gesturing shadows. Repeating patterns. Drumbeats on the wind.

The Swearingens knew what had been done.

That field once held a burial ground for over 1,500 Miami people, many of whom had died during and after General Anthony Wayne's campaigns in the Northwest Indian War. A missionary, Father Grimes, had taken in the survivors, taught them to grow corn, and lived among them.

When he died, they buried him there, beside their own. Swearingen's father had bought the land under one condition: the graves would never be disturbed. For decades, they weren't. Until a plow broke that pact.

Now, the dead returned.

Some said the white figure was Grimes himself, rising with the Miami dead to resist the desecration. Others believed it was the settler who had made the promise, furious at its betrayal.

No matter who he was, he came back again and again.

Witnesses said the ghostly figures emerged as night fell—moving through the earth and trees, always near the boundary of the old burial rise, as if trying to warn or reclaim.

Those Who Use the Cursed Land

Today, the graves are gone.

Apartments, office buildings, highways, and restaurant patios now sit on land that once promised peace to the dead.

But the peace was broken.

And even now, those who live and work there report strange things—drums after midnight, shadows in the hall, heatless flashes of light, and, on occasion, the impression that someone is standing just outside, waiting to be let in. Watching. Waiting.

Sometimes, bad things happen to those greedy souls who do not heed them.

The land remembers. The dead do not sleep.

And a promise broken is never buried.

Hanging Man of Darrtown Pike
(Butler County)

On October 2nd and 3rd of 1851, Butler County hosted its first official agricultural fair—a modest affair held beneath a grove of withering oak trees along the Miami-Erie Canal, north of Hamilton.

There were no glowing lights, no carnival barkers, no whirling machines.

Just rows of livestock, iron-toothed implements, and crates of bruised apples and fat turnips from the season's harvest.

But to four boys from Darrtown—dirty-kneed farm kids between eight and twelve—it was a world of wonder. So they rode. Nine miles on borrowed horses. Nine miles to Hamilton.

The oldest, Taylor Marshall, was twelve, broad-shouldered and loud. With him rode Ben Scott (8), Chambers Flenner (10), and Dan Warwick (11). They stayed long past sundown.

And then they made a mistake.

They took the old road home.

Into the Hollow

The route back was Darrtown Pike—what's now Hamilton Richmond Road—a winding track that choked between dark trees and sagging hillsides. As they rode, the moon barely broke through the canopy, and the fields on either side went black.

And then came the dip.

They knew what was coming.

Hangman's Hollow.

Twenty-two years earlier, a man named Martin Koble, a stranger from Lancaster, Pennsylvania, had strung himself from a tree above the creek. Why, no one ever knew. His body rotted for days in the July sun before anyone found him. By then, wild dogs had torn into his legs.

His eyes were long gone.

Since then, the hollow has earned its name.

Some said ghosts walked there.

Others said worse things did.

What the Boys Saw

They were still mouthing half-hearted bravado when the whispering began.

Faint. Off in the trees. And then they saw it—a crowd.

Figures clustered along the road ahead, staring into the woods. The boys dismounted. Hearts pounding. Feet creeping along an overgrown path.

They crept forward.

Down into the hollow.

Into the old creek bed.

The smell hit first—meat turned rancid. Flies buzzed thick as wool. And then they saw him.

Dangling.

A man. Strung up by his own suspenders, swinging just inches above the shallow water. His head lolled at an unnatural angle. His tongue protruded, black and swollen. His face looked melted—pecked raw, shredded by birds, and gnawed by field rats. One eye was gone entirely. The other hung loose, a dull marble staring through a mask of decay.

Someone whispered, "Stockman."

He'd left the fair with a purse full of cash.

He'd never made it home.

Ambushed.

Robbed.

Stripped.

Hung up like bait.

His legs were bare to the knees, his boots missing, one hand clutching at nothing, stiff with death.

The boys stared until they couldn't. Then one vomited. Another bolted. Someone saw them and shooed them away with a scolding holler. The boys left. Numb. Frightened. Somber. They didn't speak for miles.

What the Earth Gave Back

They buried him quick.

Shallow.

Right where Gardner Road runs today.

But the ground didn't keep him.

In the early 1900s, a work crew digging a culvert cracked into something beneath the soil. Bones. Boots. A rusted belt buckle. A skull with teeth still bared in death.

And still, he wasn't done.

The Ghost at the Dip

To this day, those who travel the slope where the hollow curves low say they've seen him.

Not clearly.

Just a shape—a hunched, lurching figure rising from the shadows. Sometimes, with something trailing from the stockman's throat. Sometimes pointing.

They say he's not there to haunt.

They say he warns. Warns you to stay out of the woods. Warns you that someone's waiting.

Someone with a rope. Someone with a knife.

Someone just like the ones who found him first.

If you see him, listen. And don't look away. Because the hollow still eats what it's given. And not every traveler comes out the other side.

The Blood-Gold of the Great Trail

(Carroll County)

During the blood-soaked years of the French and Indian War, George Washington led nearly 2,000 British troops toward Fort Duquesne, a pivotal French stronghold. Word of the British advance spread swiftly through the wilderness. Native scouts reached the fort before Washington's men, and among the first orders issued by the French command was not to reinforce the garrison—but to protect the gold.

Sixteen packhorses were loaded with heavy saddlebags stuffed with gold and silver—pay for the troops and bribes for alliances. The horses vanished into the wilderness with a detail of French soldiers and native guides under strict orders: If the enemy gets too close, bury the treasure. Mark the place. And die if you must—but do not let it fall into British hands.

Then It Happened

Fort Duquesne fell on November 24, 1758.

Three days later, in the thick forests near what is now Minerva, Ohio, the fleeing French soldiers found themselves pursued along the Great Tuscarawas Trail and hunted like animals. The officer ordered the men to dig. In frantic silence, they clawed into the earth and shoved the glimmering weight into the pit. They marked it: four springs, forming a near-perfect square. An oddly shaped rock wedged into the crook of a twisted tree. A deer carved into the bark a mile east. Then the packhorses were gutted, their entrails scattered, to make them unfit for use by the enemy.

And then the British found them.

All were slaughtered—save for two. Their wounds were deep; their silence was even deeper.

These men kept the secret like a curse.

The Letter

Years passed. In 1829, a letter was discovered in a trunk, yellowed and cracked. It was written by a survivor, Henry Muselle, who died in obscurity, raving in French, afraid of "shadows in the trees."

The letter gave clues to the location of the treasure.

But it also hinted at something darker: that none who buried it rested easy. The men had sworn an oath. Some had died obeying. Some had been killed because they tried to betray it.

And some, it seemed, had never truly died at all.

Muselle's nephew came searching, armed with the letter. He found the forked tree and the deer carving. Locals recalled stories—trees that bled when cut, muskets wrapped in rotting leather beneath split logs, the sound of water running from four directions toward a black center where nothing grew. But the gold never surfaced.

The Commercial newspaper in Minerva published the tale in 1875. That spring, men scoured the woods with shovels, spades, and greed in their hearts. But again, nothing. Or perhaps... no one who found it ever came back.

The Search for Treasure

Those who've searched claim more than disappointment followed them. Strange shapes have been seen between the trees—figures in colonial coats, pale hands reaching from nowhere. Shovels go missing. Compass needles spin. One man reported turning to find footprints behind him—bare feet, damp and muddy—though he was utterly alone. Another heard breathing behind his ear. When he fled, his boots stuck in mud that hadn't been there the day before.

The springs still bubble.

The deer carving is said to reappear on trees long since cut down.

And those four points where water runs? Some say they converge on something buried deep and foul-smelling. But those who've dug there claim the ground turns harder than stone. One man said it bled.

Some believe it's cursed. Others claim the gold was taken by devils wearing the faces of dead men. But most agree on this:

The treasure may still lie buried in that cursed stretch of forest...

But someone from the past—one of the soldiers, or something that wore their face—doesn't want it found.

Not now.

Not ever.

And it's still watching.

Waiting.

Protecting what was never meant to be unearthed.

Not by living hands.

Not in this world.

But still... some will try.

God help them. And goodbye.

Lincoln Ghost Train
(Champaign County)

A Nation in Mourning

On the night of April 14, 1865, President Abraham Lincoln was shot in the back of the head by John Wilkes Booth while attending a play at Ford's Theatre. He died the next morning. By April 21, his body had been embalmed and placed in a coffin lined with lead and velvet. A nine-car funeral train was prepared to carry him from Washington, D.C., back to Springfield, Illinois, for burial.

It retraced the same route Lincoln had taken on his way to the presidency—but this time, in reverse.

Thirteen days. Over 1,600 miles.

And one rotting corpse.

The Death Train

The train stopped in every major city. Not only to allow thousands of mourners to glimpse the flag-draped coffin—but to preserve what remained.

Embalming was primitive. The body bloated.

The face darkened. The tongue swelled, and fluids leaked. At each stop:

• They changed the flowers.

• Drained the rot.

• Scraped the tongue clean with a scalpel.

• Re-packed ice beneath the coffin lid.

He had to look like a president. Even in death.

Urbana, Ohio – April 29, 10:40 p.m.

The train arrived late in the evening. Nearly 10,000 people lined the tracks near North Main Street where the old depot once stood. They waited in silence.

The black-draped funeral car slowed to a stop.

Gas lamps flickered. The scent of lilies mixed with coal smoke. Twenty minutes passed.

Then, it vanished into the night.

They Say It Still Comes

Every year, on the night of April 29, Urbana falls still.

Some hear a distant whistle—long, mournful, bone-thin.

Some see the lights—a pale flicker floating above the rails.

Some see the train itself.

The same dark engine.

Same coffin car.

Same ghostly crew.

No conductor. No passengers.

Only a long box in the center car, veiled in black and oozing shadow.

And in some homes, clocks stop.

For twenty minutes.

Just like they did in 1865.

It still travels.

It still stinks of death.

And it still comes to Urbana. And then it disappears.

The Dead Man in the House Waits
(Clark County)

Daniel Hertzler was a wealthy Mennonite settler, a man of stern features and quiet resolve who came west from Pennsylvania to carve out a legacy in Clark County, Ohio. With his wife Catherine and their ten children, he built not only a successful farming estate but also sawmills and a brick distillery. As president of the Clark County Bank, he was known to keep substantial sums of cash close at hand—perhaps too close.

His large white brick home sat like a silent sentinel on the rise, overlooking the remnants of a Shawnee village. It was a house with thick walls and darker corners, and it was whispered that Hertzler never trusted banks to hold all his money. Some say he kept more than one coin locked within his cellar.

The Night They Came

On the freezing, starless night of October 10, 1867, just after 3 a.m., shadows crept across the Hertzler homestead. Four men—desperate, hungry, and armed—broke inside. Catherine, awakened by the first crash of entry, snatched up a shawl and ran barefoot into the dark to summon help, leaving behind a sleeping child in a nearby room and her husband unguarded.

By 5 a.m., neighbors arrived to a horror.

Daniel Hertzler lay dead—slumped where he had stood to defend his home. His body was cold, blood seeping in rivulets across the floorboards. His leg had been shredded by a blast of shot, his face bruised and ashen. The cradle, just a room away, still rocked slightly, the baby crying into the dawn. The family's buggy was found abandoned in Urbana the next day. And with it, the trail of justice fell silent.

Justice Escapes

Henry Roberts, found in bloodied clothing at the Union House in Bellefontaine, carried a pistol caked in residue and a sack of shot that matched the pattern embedded in Hertzler's flesh. Yet he escaped custody, and so did the other suspects. No trial. No verdict. No reckoning. They got away with it.

The House That Wouldn't Sleep

Daniel Hertzler was buried at Ferncliff Cemetery beneath a towering monument, his name etched deep in stone. In life, he had been a man of order, of discipline. In death, he became something else entirely.

Something patient.

The cemetery is peaceful. Birds warble. The grass is neatly trimmed. Visitors speak in whispers. But back at the old house above the Shawnee village—the air grows heavy come October.

Windows slam shut on still days. Footsteps echo where none should walk. And those brave—or foolish— enough to peer toward the parlor window after dark have all reported the same thing:

A pale man standing inside.

His clothes are the fashion of another century. His face is drawn tight in death's memory. And his eyes—wide, unblinking, fixed on the lawn beyond.

What He Waits For

He waits. Not with rage. Not with sorrow.

But with that quiet resolve, he once wore in life, twisted now by betrayal and blood.

He is not looking for help. He is not watching the living. He is waiting for the man who took his life and who never paid. And when they return—not in the flesh, but in time, when all debts are called— he will be there.

At the window. Waiting. Smiling.

With a shotgun full of justice and hell behind his eyes.

Smoke, Oaths, and Ghosts
(Clermont County)

Those who walk the Little Miami Scenic Trail near Miamiville sometimes glimpse it: a faint, amber light bobbing low along the old path where the sound of trains were heard quite often moving along the tracks.

It weaves just ahead, slipping between trees, ducking behind stones—always just out of reach.

Follow it, and it vanishes as it rounds the bend.

But not before you feel the air grow cold.

A Trap at the Curve

In July of 1863, Confederate General John Morgan led his raiders deep into Ohio. Near Miamiville, his men dismantled a section of the Little Miami Railroad at a place long feared by trainmen—a blind curve known for taking the careless.

They wedged cross-ties upright in the cattle guard, tore away rails, and lay in wait in the tall corn.

That morning, a Union train approached, carrying 150 unarmed Clinton County militia recruits, a baggage car, and three passenger cars. They were headed for Camp Dennison, just three miles away.

They never made it.

The Fireman's Final Hour

Cornelius Conway, the fireman aboard the locomotive, had just finished stoking the boiler when the ambush began.

Gunfire erupted from the cornfields. Bullets cracked against metal. Conway rushed up with his lantern, peering into the darkness beyond the engine's glow. He saw them—shadows with rifles. Confederate raiders.

Realizing the train was nearing a blind curve, he tried to adjust the pressure, hoping to power through it. But speed was no match for sabotage. The train hit the stripped rails. The locomotive jumped.

Steel screamed as cars twisted free and bodies were thrown into the brush like toys. Conway's body was found crushed beneath the engine, still clutching the mangled remains of his lantern.

Smoke, Oaths, and Ghosts

The young recruits survived with cracked bones and bruised dignity. Morgan's men pulled them from the wreckage and forced them to swear oaths never to fight again before releasing them.

But no one could forget what they saw in the flames.

What they heard as they crawled from the rubble.

Some claimed they heard the scream of a man still inside the wreck—screaming even after he should have been dead.

A Lantern in the Fog

They buried Conway, but the trail never forgot him.

Not long after, people began to report a dim lantern flickering along the tracks. Some said they saw a figure walking just ahead, back hunched, clothes tattered, one arm dangling at his side and the other raised high, holding a glowing light. His face—blackened, twisted, mouth frozen in an open, silent cry.

Sometimes, there's the sound of a metal shovel clanging against stone. Sometimes, a hiss of steam in the trees. And always... the curve.

The Curve That Still Waits

Even now, on fog-heavy nights, hikers feel it—a weight in the chest, the silence thick. Then comes the light, drifting through the gloom. Don't follow. Don't speak. Just step off the old tracks. Cornelius Conway is still trying to stop a train that never stops. And you don't want to be in its way.

The Dead Woman Who Watches the Graves

(Clermont County)

They Built it on Bones.

Bethel Methodist Church still stands in Southeastern Ohio's Clermont County, slumped on its old stone foundation—white boards weathered to gray, windows dimmed by decades of grime. It backs against the woods now, surrounded by brambles and silence, a forgotten corner of East Fork State Park where even the birds fall quiet.

The Earth Remembers

Long before the state took the land when the road was dirt, and the woods stretched unbroken, a preacher named John Collins rode into the frontier with fire in his voice and a Bible clutched in his fists. He built the first chapel here—a crude log thing, dark and damp. They say he preached with such fury even the devil flinched. That church is long gone, rotted to its nails.

But the bones beneath it stayed.

The white frame church that replaced it in 1818 still lingers, hollow as a ribcage. When the Army Corps came to flood the valley and carve out the park, the congregation scattered. The doors were locked. The woods crept in.

Something Stayed Behind

Visitors say they've seen her—an old woman stooped and swaying, gliding without sound between the church and the graves.

No one knows her name. No one dares to ask.

She wears a black dress wet with soil, and her veil is like gauze soaked in ash. Her face is sagging ruin—cheeks sunken, lips chewed away, eyes milk-white and bottomless.

Sometimes, she hums hymns. But it's not the tune that unsettles. It's the way the notes crawl under your skin like centipedes, wrong and broken, cracked by time and rot. Those who linger too long, joke near the stones, or wander off-trail speak of cold fingers wrapping around their wrists. Of voices that rasp from the tree line— "Don't step where they sleep."

One young woman claimed she saw her rise from an open grave, her face just inches from her, mouth a black hole twitching with worms.

The locals don't go near Bethel Methodist Church at night. They say she guards the graves. That she watches. That if you speak too loudly or forget to bow your head, she'll mark you. And when she follows, it's not fast. You'll just start hearing footsteps behind you.

Every day. A little closer.

So, keep your voice low if you walk the path by the old white church. Keep your hands out of your pockets. And if you feel something cold trail up your spine, don't turn around. Not until you leave the woods.

And don't come back. Not ever.

Glowing Grave
(Clinton County)

Along a quiet backroad outside Wilmington stands Haw Chapel Cemetery, a grove filled with ancient oaks and weathered stones. One marker, near the treeline, captures the attention of those who pass by after dark. On moonlit nights, when mist drifts low, this stone seems to emit its own light—faint, pale, and impossible to identify. Approaching it reveals nothing hidden, only the cold surface of the marble. However, when viewed from a distance, it glows like a lantern lit from within.

College Hall Haunting
(Clinton County)

In the hushed hours when the campus sleeps, some walk past College Hall only to pause at sounds that shouldn't echo inside: the unmistakable rhythm of hoofbeats and whinnies. They speak of a phantom horse—Ole Bill, entombed within the building itself. His remains were discovered during renovations in 1957, including his skull displayed in the hallway. Since then, staff report hearing a horse near the display.

The Curse Beneath the Waters of Caesar Creek
(Clinton County)

Caesar's Grave

Caesar Creek runs cold through the heart of Clinton, Greene, and Warren Counties—a long slash of water cutting across what used to be forest, homestead, and burial ground. Long before the lake swallowed the valley before roads were paved and parks laid out, the creek wound through deep ravines and shadowed hollows where something darker always seemed to wait.

They say the name comes from Caesar—an enslaved man who either fled into the wilderness with a band of Shawnee or was dragged away during one of their raids. What happened to him after that is unknown. But something terrible marked his end. His grave, they say, lies hidden in the roots and clay of the creekbed. And some nights, when the wind hisses low, and the trees tremble, you can hear a voice rise from the water. It's not like a man calling. No—it's cracked and hollow, like a throat filled with mud.

"Oh mourner, brother, you shall be free—"

It echoes like a hymn.

Like a curse.

The Pale Woman on the Banks

Before the reservoir came, the valley was quiet and untamed. Dense woods bordered the creek, and scattered farms dotted the hills. The land was fertile, but something about the place made folks uneasy. Seasons passed, and families came and went. No one stayed for long. They spoke of a ghostly woman who wandered the banks in the half-light—tall, draped in tattered white, her face too pale and far too long as if stretched with grief. Her eyes were dark hollows, her hands stained red. She didn't walk—she hovered. And when she passed, the air turned freezing cold, the birds stopped, and the forest fell silent.

Those who tried to speak to her said she looked through them as if through glass. One man claimed he touched her shoulder and pulled back a hand slick with something warm. Blood, he thought. Or worse.

She left no footprints—only withered paths where the grass curled and blackened beneath her steps.

Drowned and Not at Rest

When Caesar Creek Lake was created, the government flooded the land—burying roads, lives, graveyards, and ruins beneath the water. Homes were seized. Families scattered. But you can't drown what isn't dead. And some say those who were driven from their homes never truly left. After death, they returned—drawn back to the place that was taken from them. Now they walk the shore in silence, searching for the lives they once had.

The pale woman still walks, sometimes far from the shore. And Caesar? Some say he walks, too, though he's harder to see. Easier to *feel*.

Campers have woken to muddy footprints circling their tents. Fishermen speak of hearing splashes in the dead of night—followed by chanting that isn't quite human.

What Waits Beneath

Locals don't swim after dark. They don't walk the shore alone. Something is in the water. And the dead along Caesar Creek were never at peace—not Caesar, not the woman, not the ones buried in the hollow and forgotten when the waters rose.

Some say the creek was cursed.

Others say it remembers.

But those who have heard the voice all agree:

It doesn't call for help.

It calls for company. And it never calls just once.

The Ghost of Esther Hale at Hambleton Mill
(Columbiana County)

In the early 1800s, the Hambleton brothers—James, Charles, Benjamin, and Isaac—claimed a stretch of land near Beaver Creek and carved out the town of Sprucevale. For a while, it thrived: canal boats groaned through the locks, the grist mill screamed with grinding stone, and blacksmiths pounded iron into shape as smoke curled over the roofs of two dozen homes. But everything in Sprucevale depended on the Sandy and Beaver Canal.

And when it failed, so did the town. By 1870, Sprucevale had rotted back into the earth, a husk of moss-choked stone and hollowed doorframes.

Only the grist mill still stands at what is now Beaver Creek State Park. And a woman named Esther Hale.

She was no myth. Esther Hale belonged to the Orthodox Friends—an early preacher from Pennsylvania remembered for her temperance sermons and for working alongside the canal crews. She was tough, frugal, and often unwelcome among the men who drank hard after long days on the water. Still, she returned—again and again—urging them to "follow the path to salvation."

She vanished from the record sometime after the canal began to decline. Some say she returned east. Others say she stayed long after the others left, caring for the old mill as the roof caved in and the weeds grew tall.

But that wasn't the end.

The Return

Locals whisper that on St. Nicholas Eve—December 5th—a pale figure in white appears outside the old mill. She carries no lantern. She makes no sound.

Instead, she scratches a single word onto the stone wall of the mill: COME

Some who've seen her swear she turns, glances once over her shoulder, then drifts through the doorway and disappears. If you follow, the door to the mill groans open.

Some do.

No one sees what happens once they cross the threshold. The air shifts. The dark thickens.

But press your ear to the cold stone on a still night, and you'll hear her beneath the floorboards—

A voice, cracked and wet with rot, whispering through the grit:

"Follow me down the path…"

Then comes the sound of fingernails—scraping, scratching, and digging through the rock that buried her.

She's still trying to save the sinners.

Still trying to drag them to salvation.

And that might be fine—if your soul is clean.

But if it isn't?

Run.

Run before she sees you.

Because this time, she isn't preaching.

She's pulling you down with the rest of them.

The Bloody End of Pretty Boy Floyd and the Frightening Beginning of a Ghost
(Columbiana County)

Charles Arthur Floyd—nicknamed "Pretty Boy" for his baby face and devil-may-care charm—wasn't born an outlaw. He was a farm boy from Oklahoma, raised in red clay and dust storms, starved by the Great Depression. But the banks took everything—land, dignity, blood— and in return, Floyd took to robbing them.

He was no simple thief. He was a symbol. To the poor, he became a folk hero. To the law, he was a menace with a .45 and a growing body count. For nearly a year, he vanished into the backwoods and backroads, hiding in barns and bootlegger shacks, sleeping under newspaper with a gun on his chest.

But in October 1934, his luck and time ran dry.

Dust and Debt

The summer of '34 baked the Ohio River Valley until the soil cracked like old leather. In the flint-hard fields around East Liverpool, every breath tasted of drought and bank notes gone sour. Charles Arthur "Pretty Boy" Floyd—once a boy hoeing cotton under an Oklahoman sun—had become a wraith on the backroads, drifting from safehouse to safehouse with the smell of gun oil and burnt paper clinging to his coat.

Each time he burst through a marble-floored bank lobby, he would slash open the vault, grab the cash, and burn mortgage documents—those signed death warrants that left families homeless. Homeowners cheered; sheriffs cursed; creditors watched their power burn to ash. But charity has its cost. Blood. Lots of it.

The Hunt

By autumn, Hoover's Bureau wanted him displayed in chains—or dead and silent beneath the cornstalks. Agents trailed rumor after rumor: a stolen Ford idling outside a hobo camp in Weirton, a flask left behind in a moonshiner's shack near Steubenville, a half-burned bundle of canceled mortgages drifting along the Ohio River like black petals.

On October 22, the net closed. Floyd was spotted eating fried chicken in Wellsville's Rose Café—nervous eyes flicking to every window. Two locals tipped off the feds. Within an hour, agents Melvin Purvis and Herman "Ed" Hollis were rattling down State Route 213, Tommy guns clattering on the floorboards, fury on their tongues.

Blood in the Corn

They cornered him on the Conkle farm at dusk, on Sprucevale Road about 2 miles south of Clarkson and near Wellsville, just west of East Liverpool. Cornfields stood ragged and skeletal, ears shriveled by the long dry spell—knife-edged leaves hissing in the wind like a crowd of gossips. Floyd broke for the rows, mud sucking at his boots. The agents opened fire.

Bullets stitched across the stalks, tearing green to ribbons, spitting dirt and kernel shards into the air.

He fell once—got up—fell again. A slug punched through his right lung, and another shattered his hip. When he dropped for the last time, he clutched the earth as if digging himself a grave with his fingernails. Corn husks soaked up his blood until they looked like wilted red lilies. One agent swore the dying outlaw tried to speak—a name, a prayer, or maybe another bank's worth of debts he still yearned to erase—but the only sound was wet gurgling and the rasp of wind through broken stalks.

The Restless Road

A bronze plaque marks the spot today, bolted to a rough stone that sinks deeper each year. Yet travelers swear a second memorial roams the two-lane blacktop after dark.

Some say if you drive that road at night, especially near October 22, you'll see him. An emaciated figure in a threadbare suit limps along the shoulder, one hand pressed to a ruinous chest wound, the other clutching an invisible ledger aflame with ghost fire.

He's dressed in torn brown slacks and a bloodstained shirt.

When headlights hit him, his face lights up—a waxy, dead thing. Jaw slack. Eyes sunken, wide, staring straight ahead like he's still running. Still trying to get away.

He doesn't speak. He doesn't wave. But he stops. And he listens.

If your car engine coughs.

If your tires slow.

If you hesitate, even for a second…he turns.

And you'll see the hole.

Right through his chest. Black, wet, and open.

Like it's waiting to be filled.

With breath.

With blood.

With someone else's heart.

He stops. Turns. Listens.

Because some debts don't end with death.

And some men don't stay buried.

Crying Matilda: Blood in the Cistern

(Coshocton County)

Roscoe was once a thriving port along the Ohio and Erie Canal—a place built on grain, sweat, and slow-moving water. In the autumn of 1848, the town bustled with the sounds of trade, canal traffic, and industry. But one building along the main street—half apothecary, half residence—would soon be remembered for something far darker.

Inside lived a druggist and his wife, Matilda Wade. On a quiet September day, Matilda descended to the basement to scrub the week's washing.

She never returned.

When a neighbor entered hours later to use the same washroom, she noticed something wrong. The floor was slick with blood—fresh, glistening puddles that glinted in the dim light. A thin smear led away, disappearing into a shadowed corner of the stone wall.

There, behind an old shelf and tangled cobwebs, sat a dry, unused cistern. Its lid was askew.

The neighbor screamed for help. When Matilda's husband arrived, he refused to wait. With shaking hands and a rope tied around his waist, he was lowered into the black pit.

He didn't scream—he only gasped. Then vomited.

Matilda's body lay crumpled at the bottom, soaked in filth and runoff. Her head had been nearly hacked from her spine—sawn down to the gristle and left dangling by strands. One eye was still open. Her white laundry apron was soaked red and clinging to her like a second skin.

A Madman's Blade

John Gearhart, a stable boy and handyman, had been seen loitering near the building. His axe—still sticky with blood—was found behind the barn, and his coat reeked of rot and iron. He claimed he remembered nothing. That something "got in his head" and made him do it.

They said he laughed when the judge pronounced him guilty by reason of madness.

He died coughing blood in a prison cot months later—cholera ate his guts, but not fast enough.

Still, She Weeps

And yet, Matilda Wade never rested.

The cistern was sealed, but people said it leaked in the rain—long after it should've dried. Some heard sobbing echo down the alley behind the old building.

Faint.

Wounded.

Unrelenting.

Others glimpsed a pale figure hunched over the bricks, her face buried in bloodless hands, her white dress billowing without wind.

She never looked up.

Because her killer may have rotted—but justice never came. Not really.

And in Roscoe, that kind of unfinished business doesn't stay buried.

Especially not in a hole dug for the dead, which is covered but still present behind the old building. So too is Matilda Wade, still sobbing.

Dead Man Hollow
(Crawford County)

In the autumn of 1836, the air turned cold early in the Alleghenies. Two men set out on foot from Pennsylvania—John Hammer, 45, a married farmer looking for new land to buy, and his younger brother-in-law, Daniel Bender, only 25, unmarried and full of restless energy. John carried $200 in savings, hidden in a pouch sewn into the lining of his coat. Daniel carried just over $30 and not much more than the naive trust of a young man chasing freedom.

They passed through Wooster, Ohio, stopped at a bank, and bought provisions in Galion. There, they met two men loitering near a grocer's door—travelers, they claimed, heading west on the same road. They were friendly enough. Offered to join the journey for company. For "protection," one joked.

By the time they reached the swampy flats of the Olentangy, the road narrowed to two muddy deer trails threading through thick cane and wet brush. The four walked in pairs—Daniel and one stranger, John and the other—as the trail split along a marsh feeding into the black waters of Whetstone Creek.

The woods held their breath.

Without warning, the stranger behind Daniel drew a pistol and blew the back of his head open. Blood sprayed the wet leaves. Daniel collapsed face-first into the bog, dead before the gunpowder cleared. At the exact moment, the man behind John swung a club-sized branch, splitting the back of his skull and sending him crashing into the mud.

John didn't die.

 Not yet.

He regained consciousness in a pool of blood and rainwater. His limbs were trembling, his tongue thick with the taste of copper and dirt. Somehow, he stumbled into a sawmill down the road. The workers didn't understand his German, but they saw the blood. They saw the horror.

By the time they reached the swamp, Daniel's body had vanished beneath the muck.

It would be hours before someone stumbled upon it, his features distorted, his scalp peeled like bark, and half his money gone. The murderers were never caught.

The trail grew cold. The woods went quiet, like nothing ever happened. But the hollow never rested. It clutched the blood and violence in its roots. And it never let go.

The Ghost on the Road

They still call it Dead Man Hollow—a stretch of ground where nothing grows quite right. Trees lean away from the creek. Fog hangs too long after sunrise.

Years later, a father raced down the same path in a horse-drawn buggy, his daughter burning with fever in his arms. From the roadside, a gaunt stranger with hollow eyes and skin like old candle wax stepped from the trees and raised a pale hand.

"Your girl won't last the night," he whispered.

The father lashed the reins in panic, and the carriage sped away. But by nightfall, the girl was dead, her mouth frozen mid-scream. The father swore it until his dying breath: the man on the road was Daniel Bender.

He came back. But was it to warn... or to curse?

If you walk the woods near the old swamp trail, you may feel him. Something cold behind your back. A presence that doesn't blink. And if you ever get lost in the hollow and hear footsteps in the mud behind you—don't turn around. Daniel's still there. Still bleeding. Still watching.

And no one knows if he's trying to save you—or drag you under.

The Overcrowded Bones At Woodland Cemetery

(Cuyahoga County)

The Unearthed

In February of 1854, James Lawrence purchased a large lot at Woodland Cemetery. It remained vacant for nearly a year until Lawrence authorized the burial of a man named Joseph Tomkins. No record explains their relationship. Tomkins, approximately 39 years old, had lived on York Street in Cleveland and died of consumption.

The gravediggers heaped soil high upon the mound—but no marker was placed. The grass eventually grew. The grave all but disappeared.

No visitor ever came. No one asked about Joseph Tomkins. Only the yellowed cemetery records bore silent witness to his presence beneath the ground.

The Encroachment

Twenty years passed. The Lawrence family sold the lot to Jacob Hofman, unaware—or unwilling to admit—that a body was already buried beneath the earth. When Hofman's relatives began to die, gravediggers disturbed the soil to prepare more plots. That was when the peace unraveled. The restless dead do not take kindly to the intrusion.

A Spirit's Plea

In 1912, Mary Pauli—a 62-year-old spiritualist—attended a séance, as she often did. There, the medium stopped suddenly. A spirit had been lingering, they said, waiting for Mary. His name was Joseph Tomkins. Once a doctor—distinguished, dark-haired, dressed in gray with a military cape—he had a single, desperate plea: "Find my grave... and make sure it is clearly marked."

His bones had rotted. His name had faded. But the injustice burned on.

The Discovery

Mary Pauli went to Woodland Cemetery and combed the records with staff. Joseph Tomkins was indeed buried in the Hofman family plot, unmarked, forgotten. She paid for a modest headstone, believing her duty was fulfilled. But peace never lasts.

The Exhumation

When the Hofmans discovered flowers on the plot, they demanded an explanation. The cemetery staff confirmed the burial, but tensions rose. Permission was given to exhume the grave.

December 26: Two diggers, August Schmiel and John Palluch, unearthed coffin fragments, a tall skeletal frame, and a skull with dark hair and leathery tissue still clinging to the bone.

The remains were forced into a three-foot box, nailed shut, and relocated to a pauper's row among the unclaimed and unnamed.

The Disturbance

January 3: Mary Pauli returned to the medium. The spirit of Joseph Tomkins came again—but this time, in agony:

"I am miserable—worse off than before. They twisted me into a cramped box. My legs are upside down. I cannot rest. Please help me!"

The next day, she demanded answers from the cemetery staff. "He lay undisturbed for 58 years. He should not have been moved." But unless she paid for a new casket and premium plot, they would do nothing.

The Bare Spot

And so Joseph Tomkins was left—his bones twisted in a narrow grave. Final records show the body was moved to Section: 83 Lot: Tier: 5 Grave: 44 with a simple wooden marker, now gone. Now, even that is gone.

Nothing remains but a bare spot in the grass.

The Obsession

But that was not the end.

Deep beneath the ground, amidst the rotted bones and decayed skull long eaten by beetles and maggots, the corpse still reached out to the living, begging those who are sensitive to the dead to his proper burial ground. I know. When I discovered this old story in a worn, brown-edged newspaper, something stirred within my mind. It clung fiercely like a dog's gaze following a tossed bone with meat still attached.

I found his name and combed the brittle records. I chased it with growing fixation. I traced old burial logs and walked row after row through rain and sun. Something gnawed at me.

A tug, subtle at first. Then undeniable.

It was as if he had been reaching up all along—into my thoughts, my dreams—coaxing me closer. Joseph Tomkins did not want peace.

He wanted attention.

The Thirst

At last, I found the unmarked patch—bare dirt, no stone, no flowers. I stood alone above the cramped box and felt the earth pulse as though something beneath was breathing slow, rancid breaths. That's when I understood: Tomkins never wanted peace. He wants witnesses. This ghost, this thing that used to be a man— he was drawing people in. Not to be remembered.

To be fed. Fed by thought. By sympathy. By fear. Every mind that turned his name over gave him strength.

And maybe that thirst won't stop until someone else lies beside him.

Dead.

Or nearly.

So I backed away with my heart pounding, just as Mary Pauli had done before me. And maybe more between us. And now it's your turn to wonder what lies beneath that grass. Just hope he hasn't chosen you.

Because some thirsts aren't quenched. They grow. They wait.

And sometimes... they reach back.

Walk away, I beg you.

Just walk away.

Blood in the Ravine: The Mad Butcher of Kingsbury Run
(Cuyahoga County)

During the depth of the Great Depression, Cleveland's east-side gorge known as Kingsbury Run—all jagged quarries, sewer-thick creek water, and ragged rail lines— became a shantytown of the desperate. Tar-paper shacks and scavenged boxcars clung to the slopes, smoke curling from oil-drum stoves. By night, the ravines filled with coughing, whispered deals, and the dull clang of freight trains rolling overhead.

A Killer Steps From the Shadows (1934–1938)

Into this misery walked an artist of dismemberment that the newspapers christened "The Mad Butcher of Kingsbury Run."

At least a dozen drifters, sex workers, and hoboes vanished into the darkness. Each was decapitated—often while still breathing—and their heads were taken as trophies.

Torsos surfaced in weeds and culverts or tangled in river drift. At the same time, arms, legs, and severed heads appeared miles away, bundled in newspaper and burlap like spoiled meat.

Police compared the precision to a slaughterhouse floor—or a medical theater where someone practiced with scalpels and bone saws instead of cleavers.

The First to Surface: "Lady of the Lake"

On a wind-bitten September morning in 1934, twenty-one-year-old Frank La Gossie combed Euclid Beach for scrap wood. He spotted what he thought was a pale fish belly protruding from the sand, yanked it free, and nearly fainted—a female torso, arms hacked off at the shoulders, legs clipped just below the knees, head gone.

Reporters named her Lady of the Lake. Though not always counted among the Butcher's victims, her slaughtered remains matched his signature.

Surgery by Moonlight

Victim after victim followed—dumped beneath the Kinsman Road bridge, wedged in sewer pipes, or afloat in the Cuyahoga's oily current.

The coroner whispered of clean intercostal cuts and vertebrae separated "as neatly as a textbook illustration." Whoever wielded the blade knew how to peel a body like an orange to get to the tender meat beneath.

Large, right-handed, and strong enough to shoulder limp corpses. Charismatic enough to lure the hungry and half-frozen back into the dark. Practiced enough to work fast—no screams ever reported.

By August 1938, police hauled the final two torsos from the Lakeshore Dump, ribs sawn apart like picket fences. Then the murders stopped—as if the killer simply folded his knives and stepped offstage.

Kingsbury Run Today

The shacks burned long ago. City crews bulldozed the ravine in a futile attempt to scour its memory, yet the tracks still hum, and weeds still claw through broken pavement. Night breezes carry a sour reek of cinders and rot that no reclamation ever erased.

Locals swear the Butcher's shade still prowls these gullies, watching the homeless camps under the freeway ramps, yearning for flesh that will not be missed.

And sometimes—on fog-heavy nights—drifters claim they see shapes assembling downstream: headless silhouettes wading out of the Cuyahoga, amassing piece by piece, marching back to the places where they were unmade.

But far worse, at times they note something dark and hulking hovering above them. The Butcher sniffing the wind ready to return and carve once again.

The Ghost in the Mill
(Darke County)

Gabriel Baer built the water-powered gristmill in 1850, carving it into the wooded edge of Greenville Creek like a secret meant to last. The stone walls were quarried by hand. The giant millstones—each weighing over 1,200 pounds—were hauled in by oxen. And from the moment the first gears turned, it became the beating heart of the countryside. Through war, famine, and flood, the old mill stood. Grinding wheat into flour. Corn into meal.

Generations passed through its heavy doors, tracking in dust and carrying out sustenance.

But the one who never left was Baer himself.

The mill thrived under his care, and locals claimed he could tell the quality of grain just by smell. He was meticulous. Tireless. Some said obsessed. When he died, the building groaned without him.

The waterwheel slowed.

The stones cooled.

But not for long.

Since the 1970s, when the last commercial bag was milled, and the Friends of Bear's Mill took over, something else has stirred inside.

Footsteps in the Flour Dust

Visitors speak of the sound first—a soft shuffle across the boards upstairs. Not heavy. But measured. Like a man walking with purpose.

When they turn, there is no one there.

Then comes the scent.

Not of grain.

Not of oil or grease, nor the cool, damp stone.

But scorched flour.

Burnt.

As if something went wrong in the gears. As if someone stayed too long at the wheel.

Lights flicker. Doors close. A shadow lingers on the stairs beside the old grain bins. And when the mill is empty—truly empty—you can sometimes hear a low grinding noise with no one near the stone.

The Defiance Werewolf: The Summer of '72
(Defiance County)

Hairy and Howling

Defiance, Ohio—a quiet town folded between the Maumee and Auglaize Rivers—has seen its share of history. General "Mad" Anthony Wayne built a fort here in the late 1700s. Railroads came in the 1800s, bringing bustle and soot and the grinding metal rhythm of industry. But it wasn't until 1972 that Defiance earned something far stranger.

That summer, under July and August moons, a beast arrived. Not just any beast. A hulking, hairy, fanged, club-wielding thing that stalked the train depot and residential streets in the dark hours between midnight and dawn. It wasn't a man. And it wasn't just a dog. It was both—and it was angry. Witnesses didn't hesitate. Seven to eight feet tall. Raggedy clothes. Fangs. A club in its fist.

The Cops Took It Seriously

At first, Defiance police suspected a robber in costume. But Chief Breckler was not amused. "Very hairy is the first description given by each person who saw the werewolf," he told reporters. "We don't think it is a prank. He's coming at people with a club in his hand. We think it's to the safety of our people to be concerned."

"It Had Huge Hairy Feet"

This wasn't a drunk with a gorilla mask.

The thing showed up under a full moon at 4 a.m.—twice. Brakemen Tom Jones and Ted Davis were working the N&W overnight local freight when they came face to fangs with it. The beast didn't creep. It stomped. Side to side. Slow and brutish. Davis recalled: "I was connecting an air hose between two cars and was looking down. I saw these huge hairy feet, then I looked up, and he was standing there with that big stick over his shoulder. When I started to say something, he took off for the woods."

Jones, who had previously mocked Davis for the tale, wasn't laughing later. "At first, I thought the whole thing was a big joke, but when I saw how hairy and woolly it was—that was enough for me."

More reports followed.

A woman's doorknob twisted under a hairy hand. A grocery clerk driving home spotted it in his headlights at 4 a.m. Same size. Same stench. Same savage teeth.

One man claimed the creature wore jeans and moved like it remembered being human—but hadn't quite figured it out yet.

Then, as suddenly as it appeared, the thing vanished. No body. No blood. Just gouged fenceposts, shaken railroaders, and a deep hush that settled over Defiance like steam off the rails.

To this day, no one knows what walked those tracks.

A werewolf? A prankster in a Halloween costume? Some half-evolved thing dragged from the caves of time?

Or maybe it wasn't hunting at all—perhaps it was just trying to catch the last train home.

The Red Slipper Murder
(Delaware County)

A Face Beyond Recognition

September 1953. A squirrel hunter crept through the scrub along Route 53—three miles north of Upper Sandusky, Ohio—when he found what looked like a pile of laundry discarded near a gravel turnout.

But it was no bundle.

It was a girl.

She lay crumpled in the weeds, dressed in nothing but a thin flannel nightgown and red, one-strap slippers.

Her face had been pulverized—beaten so violently it no longer resembled something human. The blood had dried in sheets down her neck, her mouth gaping, frozen mid-scream.

There was no identification. No name. No purse. Just the shoes.

The Slippers That Spoke

One of the detectives turned the slipper over. A serial number.

It traced back to Prima Footwear in Columbus. From there, to a department store in White Plains, New York. Police arrived, photo in hand. A clerk remembered selling the slippers just two days before a blue-eyed girl named Cynthia Pfeil vanished.

She was nineteen. Pregnant. And gone.

The Boy With the Lead Pipe Smile

Cynthia's parents said she had been seeing a boy they didn't trust. Roger Schinagle—a clean-cut college kid from Ohio Wesleyan, all charm and sand-colored hair. He worked for a trucking company. Drove through Cleveland to see her.

But Cynthia had returned home that summer and something was different. She was quiet. Nervous. She said she had something to tell him and traveled to Delaware, Ohio. She never made it back.

Roger didn't take her to a hotel. He locked her in a university equipment shed behind the south athletic fields.

And he kept her there.

When a groundskeeper spotted the girl wandering nearby, Roger lost control. He dragged her back into the dark, beat her until she was senseless, then wrapped his hands around her throat until she stopped moving.

But that wasn't enough. He took a lead pipe and smashed her face. Seventeen blows.

Not rage—removal.

He didn't want anyone to recognize what was left of her.

Buried Twice

Roger dumped her body in the tall weeds along Route 53 and went back to class. They arrested him within days. He confessed. The court gave him ten years. Cynthia got a casket in White Plains. Her unborn child went in with her. But rest did not come.

Henry Street Haunting

They say she still walks. Not near the shed. Not in White Plains. But along Henry Street, close to where she died—where the blood soaked into the dirt and the red slippers came to a stop.

Drivers report a figure at the edge of the road: pale, barefoot, hands curled at her sides.

Some say she cries. Some say she calls for help.

But others say she does neither. She stares—blank-faced and twisted, a dark dented mask where a girl once smiled. Her eyes glint in the headlights. Her lips never move. And when she turns to walk, the red slippers leave no prints. Only blood in the gravel.

Kelleys Island: The Ice Never Gave Them Back

(Erie County)

Kelleys Island and Middle Island rise like quiet sentinels in the dark waters of Lake Erie, their shores whispered about for more than a century. The lake holds many things—shipwrecks, secrets, and strange lights that shimmer just above the waves. Some say the lights belong to late-night fishermen or passing boats, their lanterns blurred by mist and distance. But not all the lights behave that way.

Bootlegger's Island

Some blink in unnatural rhythms. Some vanish the moment they're spotted. And some linger—just offshore or drifting near the barren rock of Middle Island—without a source. Locals had passed them off as bootleggers' beacons or smugglers' tricks from the Prohibition years when men like Toledo gangster Joe Roscoe ran rum from Canada to Ohio under cover of night. His hideaway—once a casino and resort on Middle Island called the Lake Erie Fishing Club—was razed long ago. But something of him remains. And something else. Old-timers say the lights began to change after March 1, 1926.

Lost in the Storm

That night, James Phipps, his wife Lula, and their three children—two-year-old Elmer, six-year-old Hazel, and seven-year-old Paul—left Pelee Island in their sedan and headed for Leamington. The lake had frozen solid weeks before, and locals often used the ice as a road when weather allowed. But the night turned. A blizzard swept in like a curtain. The sky fell into the earth. And the Phipps family vanished.

The Sound of the Dead Being Searched For

They say you could hear the searchers for miles—horns and whistles sounding over the ice like calls to the dead. Axes hammered against the lake. Saws cut trenches. Men shouted names into the white. But there was nothing. No vehicle. No broken ice.

No signs of life.

Then, the lights came.

They flickered across Middle Island—though the lighthouse there had been abandoned a year before. Glowing like torches seen through a fogged window, the lights pulsed just long enough to lure boats closer.

The Fog That Shouldn't Have Been There

Some searchers swore they saw fires on the island's edge. Others heard faint voices. But when they arrived—there was no ash. No footprints. Only snow.

On the return trip, an unnatural fog rolled in from the east, low and fast. It smothered the boats, swallowed their engines, and turned the compass dials without touching them. For a moment, one search party believed they were circling the same stretch of black water. The same ice. Over and over.

The Thaw and the Truth

It wasn't until the thaw that James Phipps floated to the surface, miles from where they'd last seen him. Then came Lula, Elmer, and Hazel—pulled from the lake like dolls from a forgotten grave.

But Paul... Paul was never found.

The Lights That Stayed

Either way, the lights have never stopped.

They still flicker off the coast of Middle Island, pulsing brighter in winter, or during storms, or when the lake churns cold and gray. A few have followed them, hoping to uncover gold, or old Prohibition liquor, or the final truth of what happened to the Phipps family.

But the island keeps its dead. And the lights? They're still calling someone home.

Half-calf Shade of Stillhouse Hollow
(Fairfield County)

Long before Lancaster spread its limbs into tidy roads and brick storefronts, a rugged path twisted beside a stream called Fetters Run. It cut through the old farms—Foglesong, Spangler, Fetters—and trailed behind the Poor House Farm, finally ending near what is now Rising Park. Its path now roughly follows Stringtown Road, but it was formerly known as Foglesong Road after the family whose farm abutted a large portion of the road.

Cries in the Dark

Along a place called Flat Rocks, a deep and dark ravine split the land like an open wound. Locals called it Still-House Hollow—due to the inconspicuous whiskey shack once nestled in the glen. The still was long gone, but something had soaked into the dirt and never left. Screams echoed from the hollow at night—sickly, high-pitched cries like something halfway between animal and man. Travelers complained of a pressure in their chest, of the air turning to syrup, of a crushing dread they couldn't name.

The Horrifying Ride

And then came Jacob Spangler.

He was known as a steady man. On a cold autumn night in the mid-1800s, he saddled his mare to fetch the doctor for a fevered child. As he descended the forested hill into Still-House Hollow, his horse locked up—quivered so hard the bridle jingled. She refused to take another step.

Spangler peered ahead. At first, he saw nothing but darkness and the shadows of branches. Then it shifted. A figure in the road.

A calf.

No—a *thing* like a calf. But it stood wrong. Its eyes glowed green and glassy like rotted marbles. Long, matted hair clung to its sides. The stench of rot filled the air. Spangler raised his reins to wheel around—and that's when something grabbed his leg.

He looked down.

IT WAS CRAWLING UP HIM.

The Half-calf Shade

A creature, half-man, half-calf, slick with gore and black slime, pulled itself onto the horse. Its face was that of a young cow—warped and half-rotted, lips peeled back in a stiff, unnatural grin, as if it had died mid-scream and never stopped grinning. Cloven hooves. Wisps of hair. A slick, pink tongue lolled out and snorted, ending in a ghastly, almost childlike giggle.

Spangler froze. The thing climbed higher until it sat behind him in the saddle—its hooves clasped over his shoulders like a child's arms. Its breath smelled like blood curdled with bile.

The stench hit him like a blow—mungy rot and blood-soaked fur—so thick and vile it curled in his throat, made his eyes burn, and caused him to gag.

They rode together, silent. Horrifyingly, heart-pumping, tingly-fingered, numb-cheeked silence. Not until the horse broke past the edge of the hollow did the thing slide off—silent and slick—and vanish into the trees.

It left behind a stench that clung to the air like pus on bone... something long dead and something older than death itself.

Spangler sat frozen in the saddle, his chest heaving, the reins slack in his trembling hands. Sweat rolled down his temples in cold beads.

The adrenaline drained from his limbs in a wave, leaving him limp, hollowed out, as if he'd outrun the Devil himself—and only barely.

He didn't look back. He never would.

The Gruesome Truth Behind the Shade

But Spangler was not the first.

Years earlier, a man named Ornsdorff rode that same path and never came home. His horse returned without him—saddle slashed, bags torn, and a slick smear of dried brains and hair caked to the leather.

Men gathered. They followed the blood.

Up the hill. Through the trees.

Dragged marks in the grass led to a half-rotted shack beside an old whiskey still. The door was bolted, but they managed to break it.

Inside: silence.

Then—a reek that clawed its way into the throat. One man vomited.

Another bolted from the room. In the back room lay a body, gutted and splayed on the floor.

But it wasn't Ornsdorff.

It was a steer.

Split wide down the belly. Its entrails looped in piles. Its throat gaped open as if something had climbed out, not in.

The owner of the shack, an old recluse named Crowley, was never seen again. Neither was Ornsdorff. All that remained was a trail of blood that led from the body... out the back door... and into the hollow.

Some say Crowley fed the thing in the hollow.

Some say he became it.

But those were only speculations.

Nobody knows what really happened.

Stillhouse Hollow is Now Part of a Park

And still, on fog-heavy nights, when headlights sweep the woods near Keller-Kirn Park's Flat Rocks trail, some unfortunate souls report the same thing: A sudden pressure—like something sitting on their chest.

A shape twitching between the trees.

And hooves. Not on the ground. Right behind them.

In the black angles of the park's trails, people have heard screams—thin, shrill, and wet—as if someone is being torn open from the inside out.

Some say it's the dead men, still caught in their final moment.

Still thrashing. Still bleeding. Still screaming.

Others, well, they believe it is that Half-calf Shade wanting more—waiting, starving, hunting for the next warm body to finish what it started.

The Rum Rider of Muddy Prairie Run
(Fairfield County)

In the early days, when roads were nothing more than narrow, rutted traces through the wilderness, a stream called Muddy Prairie Run carved its way through the thick woods of Hocking Township in Fairfield County.

The name was no lie.

The run was sluggish and dark, fed by bogs that bled black water into the soil.

The land around it heaved and sucked underfoot, riddled with hidden mires that could take a horse down in seconds. Locals said the moss could peel skin from bone. That the earth was hungry here.

The Old Man and the Rum

Among the settlers was a bent old man with a mule as stubborn and tired as he was. Each evening, he followed the trail beside the run to a lonely distillery that squatted on the bank like a drunk clinging to the edge of a chair. He came for rum—and to tell stories.

He'd sit by the fire and spin tales long after the sun dipped, his voice soft and strange, like it wasn't always meant for human ears. He drank deep, laughed hard, and when the coals dimmed, he'd fasten his small keg to the mule and vanish into the dark.

He never missed a night. Until one night, he didn't return.

Swallowed Whole

Search parties followed the hoofprints down the path, but the trail stopped abruptly near a patch of low fog. The footprints—both man and mule—ended at the rim of a bog that had appeared where none should've been. Bubbles rose from the mud.

The water stank of rot and liquor. They never found his body. Just a corked keg bobbing against a half-submerged log.

The Vanishing Ride

Years passed. The distillery rotted into the ground. A school was built near the creek, but it was later abandoned. Houses came, and roads were paved.

But the trail along Muddy Prairie Run was never right again. And then came the sightings.

A figure on a pale, shrunken mule—both soaked in mud and mist—glides silently along the edge of the road near the old school ruins. The keg, still strapped to the saddle, leaks something dark as oil. The rider's head hangs low, jaw slack, eyes empty. If you watch too long, the mule turns—just slightly—off the trail. Into the bog.

And they vanish.

The Muck Still Moves

No one walks the creek after dark.

Not because they fear what they'll see.

Because of what they might follow.

They say if you stand by the water and listen close, you'll hear hoofbeats in the mud. Then, the creak of leather. Then... a slosh.

Like something opening.

And maybe—just maybe—your foot will slip.

And you'll understand precisely what happened to him.

Because the Run never spits out what it swallows.

And some who drink don't stagger home.

They just sink. And they are never seen again. Well, except for their ghosts.

Headless Horseman of Cherry Hill

(Fayette County)

The Hill That Keeps Its Secrets

State Route 38 near Yatesville winds past cornfields and sagging barns, but there's a place locals still won't linger after dark—a modest rise called Cherry Hill.

They say something rides there.

Something without a head.

Cherry Hill's Rotten Heart

Long before pavement and road signs, a crooked tavern sat atop Cherry Hill—little more than a lean-to of rot and whiskey breath. Its owners were a mean-mouthed couple known for watered-down drink, counterfeit coin, and the kind of backroom dealings that never left a man whole. No one trusted them. Everyone feared them.

The Man with No Face

Sometime around the frost of 1832, travelers whispered of a tall rider galloping at dusk, his head missing, his coat streaked with something dark. The horse screamed like it knew something awful. And always, the rider stopped near the tavern—then vanished into the brush.

Murder in the Cellar

It wasn't long before the story unraveled. A federal agent, sent quiet-like to investigate a counterfeiting ring, had vanished along this route. His horse was found tied to a tree behind the tavern, reins frayed from a struggle. The innkeeper had lured the man in under the guise of drink, then crushed his skull with a blacksmith's hammer. He hacked off the agent's head and shoved the body down an old well behind the smokehouse. No words. No rites. Just cold silence.

The Woman Who Talked

The innkeeper's wife found out. Maybe he confessed to her. Maybe she heard the screams. But when she threatened to turn him in, he tried to silence her too—only she fled, barefoot and bloodied, to the sheriff's door.

He was arrested by morning. She vanished soon after, no one knows where.

The Unearthing

Years later, long after the tavern burned to ash and weeds swallowed its stone foundation, a farmer turned his blade through Cherry Hill's soil. The plow struck something hard. He thought it was a stump. But it wasn't wood. It was skulls—three of them. More bones followed, twisted and snapped. One still wore rusted shackles at the ankle.

He Still Rides

They say on fog-heavy nights, the sound of hooves still echoes off the blacktop near Cherry Hill.

A rider without a head on his shoulders chases trespassers down the road, his coat billowing like smoke, his horse foaming at the mouth. Only now, he carries his head in one hand—found, but not at peace.

They say he's hunting the man who killed him.

But if you see him, don't linger.

The eyes in that dead face are moldy and rotting, and in the thick dark of the trees, he might mistake your shadow for his killer.

Something Never Left Wooly Burger Cemetery
(Franklin County)

The Thing in the Creek

Big Darby Creek runs black and cold for 84 miles, winding past the town of Darbydale like a dark vein beneath thin skin. Just outside its edge lies Little Pennsylvania Cemetery—a forgotten patch of earth where stone markers lean, inscriptions fade, and the trees seem to whisper long after dusk.

Locals call it Woolly Booger Cemetery. Or Wollyburger. Or Wooly Burger. Or sometimes, it is just that *place you don't go after dark.*

Some say the name came from an old tale—a massive, reeking creature, half-man, half-beast, with hair like moldy moss and eyes that glowed red through the pines. They say it still stalks the tree line by the creek, crouching in cattails, watching for anything that bleeds.

But others whisper a worse origin.

A man once lived near here, a quiet farmer with a good crop and a crooked grin. One night, he snapped. He slaughtered his wife and two small children with a butcher knife, then set fire to the house and hung himself from the rafters. They buried what was left of him in a family plot at the edge of the cemetery.

That was a mistake.

He came back. Twisted. Changed.

They called him the Woolly Booger, not out of folklore—but fear. And those who dared step near his grave? Some claimed they were scratched. Others shoved. One girl swore her neck bore rope burns for a week.

People thought they got the name wrong—that "Woolly Booger" was just "Willie Butcher," garbled through too many retellings. A tombstone was found: Willie Boucher, aged 1 year, 7 months.

But even if Willie never murdered anyone, someone did.

And something never left.

The Woman in the Sack

On a bitter March morning in 1957, four teenage boys casting for fish found more than trout in Big Darby Creek. The water was high and slow, dragging with it a bloated burlap feed sack snagged on a root cluster.

Inside was a dead girl.

She couldn't have been older than nineteen. Her short dark hair was slicked to her skull. She was barefoot, half-naked, strangled with a cotton clothesline wrapped three times around her neck and knotted tight enough to bite through the flesh. Her mouth was gagged. Her body cocooned in a flower-print bedspread.

They pulled her from the cold and ran.

Dr. Carl Tetirick, the acting coroner, said it plain: "Murder." She'd been dead for two days. Beautiful, perfectly proportioned, the newspapers said. But no one could name her. At the Columbus bars and dives, she'd been called Sara. Or maybe Ginny. Or Betty. Or Gerry.

Too many names. None that mattered now.

The One Who Waits

Parents warned their children after that. "Be in by dark," they'd say. "There's a monster in the woods."

And maybe that wasn't just fear talking. Even now, hikers say they've seen a man-shaped figure pacing the mowed trail behind the cemetery. Others spot it crouched by the creek, still as a stump—until it moves.

It's not Bigfoot.

It's not the ghost of the murdered girl.

It's something else.

Something that wears the dark like a coat and waits for the fog to roll in.

Some say it's the old killer returned.

Others believe it's the creek itself—Big Darby—that remembers every drowned scream and keeps them all beneath its silt.

But one thing is certain.

If you're near Little Pennsylvania Cemetery after midnight and you hear the reeds rustle or the splash of something too heavy to be a fish— don't look back.

Because IT only hunts those who notice.

And if you do?

You won't be found in one piece.

You'll be pulled from the water, wrapped in cloth, nameless.

Just like the last one.

Dragged out of the shallows.

Wrapped like meat at a butcher shop counter.

No name. No answers. Just silence.

Because Darby Creek swells with more than water.

It hides things. Keeps them.

And sometimes—it gives them back.

But not the way they went in.

Feu Follet of Goll Woods
(Fulton County)

Goll Woods is one of the last remnants of Ohio's original Black Swamp forest—dense with white oak, ash, and whispering sycamores, many of which are over 300 years old. It is in Fulton and Williams counties.

Peter and Catherine Goll settled the land after emigrating from Grand-Charmont, France, in the 1830s. Although it was cleared for farming, large portions were left wild. The Golls were known to bury their dead on the property before formal cemeteries were established.

The Goll family cemetery, now deep in the nature preserve, is small and overgrown. Some stones are broken, others vanished entirely. But it's said the spirits never left the land they built with their own hands.

Lights That Shouldn't Be

For generations, hikers and locals have reported strange floating lights in Goll Woods—especially near the old burial plots and footbridges at twilight. Described as faint blue or green flickers, they appear to hover low to the ground, drift slowly between the trees, and then vanish as suddenly as they come.

Unlike lanterns or fireflies, these lights:

- Make no sound.
- Often move against the wind.
- Sometimes, they appear in clusters, as if walking in a silent procession.

One hiker in the 1970s claimed a light followed him for nearly half a mile before disappearing near the old Goll homestead foundation.

He described it as "a pale flame that never burned, just glowed and watched."

Another visitor reported seeing two orbs rise from the ground behind the cemetery fence and then drift into the woods where no trail leads.

When he turned to check again, they were behind him.

Theories and Tradition

Pioneer Spirits: Locals say the lights are the Goll ancestors, still tending to their land—or warning intruders away from their forgotten graves.

Unmarked Dead: Others believe they're spirits of early settlers who died from illness, childbirth, or accident, buried in unrecorded places, now rising as night falls.

The Forest Itself: Some believe Goll Woods is a thin place, where the world blurs. The swampy ground and untouched trees act like a conduit—pulling in energy from beyond.

"Feu Follet" – Ghost Lights of the French Dead (will-o'-the-wisp): Another older theory refers to Feu Follet—the French term for ghostly lights of lost souls. The Goll family spoke French and Swiss-German and may have brought with them old beliefs from Europe, where such lights were thought to be wandering spirits, trapped between the living and the dead. In French folklore, "Feu Follet" appears in marshy ground or lonely woods, luring travelers away. They are not malevolent, but restless—souls denied burial rites or those who died far from home. Some say the lights of Goll Woods didn't begin in Ohio at all. They followed the Golls across the ocean—and took root in the Black Swamp forest, where the earth was soft enough to hold them.

What Remains

The Goll Woods Preserve is a quiet, beautiful place by day—but once the sun sets, it changes. The air thickens. The trees lean closer. And some say if you sit quietly near the family graves, the woods will watch you back.

And if you see a pale green light drift through the trees—don't follow. Don't speak. Just let it pass.

Old Man Mooney's Fiddle
(Gallia County)

The Road and the Hill

Long ago, travelers in carriages crept along Swan Creek Road, now called Stewart Road—a remote, crooked stretch of earth curling through the hills of Gallia County.

In those days, the road passed near Mooney Cemetery, a lonely patch of hillside ground mostly forgotten now, swallowed by forest and shadow.

But people spoke of the music.

They said that on certain nights, usually when the moon was low and the wind had gone still, a violin would begin to play. The sound came from somewhere near the cemetery—faint at first as if drifting from the trees themselves—then louder, clearer, mournful. It never played a song anyone could name. Just a slow, shivering melody that seemed to hang in the air long after the bow had stopped.

The Grave and the Musician

The story was always the same. Matthew Mooney buried his daughter Eliza there in 1854. She was five and a half when she died—too small, they said, for the box they laid her in. Something about her death twisted Matthew. He stopped speaking to neighbors. He stopped working the land. But what he did not stop was playing the violin.

He returned night after night to the grave, sat in the dirt above Eliza's headstone, and played until the crickets fell silent and the air grew cold. For a time, it was a thing of sorrow—an old man in mourning. Then, it changed.

The Dancing Spirit

People began to hear the music speeding up—notes that trilled and twisted unnaturally fast. More than one witness swore they saw a shape in the dark. A little girl. Pale. Smiling. Her feet barely touched the ground as she spun in slow circles around the grave. Her dress never moved. Her eyes never blinked.

And she was laughing. A quiet, breathless giggle that echoed across the hillside and stopped just as suddenly as it began.

Some said the ground near her headstone shifted—bulged and settled again, like something below was stirring, restless. Mooney played harder after that. More frantic. Until the night he vanished.

They found his violin a few days later, cracked in half beside Eliza's grave. The strings had been torn off and lay coiled in the grass like veins.

The Warning

The cemetery still exists, though you'd have to know where to look. The road curves past it like a body avoiding pain. Nothing marks the spot anymore but an old iron gate and some stones blackened by moss and time.

And yet, the stories persist.

People who've passed along Stewart Road on still nights claim they've heard the violin again—one single note, too long, too high. And then the giggling.

Closer than it should be.

Closer than it was.

They say some music is meant for mourning.

And some— is meant to summon the dead back.

Tangled with Pondweed
(Geauga County)

Punderson Lake is no ordinary body of water. Formed by ancient glaciers, it's the largest and deepest kettle lake in Ohio—a black, glistening eye in the wilderness. Locals swim and paddle across it every summer, never thinking about what waits beneath. But in 1977, that changed.

The Drowning

That year, a teenage girl—a quiet visitor with no swimming skills—took a canoe into the center of the lake. No one saw what caused it to tip.

Maybe she shifted wrong. Maybe something nudged it. But she went in. And she never came out.

Not alive, at least.

Her body surfaced days later. Limbs bloated. Eyes wide. Fingers curled like they'd clawed the water in her final moments. Pondweed was tangled in her hair, draped like funeral veils over her face. When they pulled her ashore, a trail of red and green followed her in the water like the lake itself was reluctant to give her up.

And maybe it didn't.

The Return

One year later, in 1978, a Romani caravan camped near the lake. The night was still but heavy—clouds low, water black and mirror-flat. The elders stood at the edge of the trees when something broke the surface.

Not a splash. A rising.

A figure appeared from the depths—slim, soaked, swaying. Her hair hung like vines, her clothing clung to her frame, and her skin was the pale gray of drowned flesh. Strips of pondweed clung to her arms. She didn't speak. She didn't blink. She simply walked ashore as if she'd never died.

And then—just as silently—she turned, walked back into the lake, and vanished.

The Romani packed up that night. Quietly. Desperately. They never returned.

She Never Left

Locals now say the girl never left. She's still beneath the surface—face-up just below the reflection, eyes open.

On fog-heavy nights, she rises. The water doesn't ripple. The frogs fall silent. Those who see her say she walks without sound, trailing wet footprints that evaporate in seconds.

But sometimes... they don't.

Some claim her ghost brushes up against boat hulls from below. That a cold hand has gripped their ankles mid-swim. That breathless panic overtakes them for no reason at all—until they scramble to shore, hearts hammering, certain they aren't alone.

Because part of her is still down there.

Waiting. Watching.

And if she drowned alone, she won't stay that way.

Not forever.

Ghost Bride of Trebein Road
(Greene County)

The Carriage and the Cold

It was a black-boned winter night in the late 1800s. A boy, dressed in borrowed finery and still flushed from the fire-lit warmth of a social gathering, was heading home in his father's rickety carriage. The horse was old— too old, maybe—and its gait lagged more with each creaking mile.

It had a way of nodding off mid-step like the weight of its years tugged at every muscle.

As the boy neared a shadowy stretch of Trebein Road, the horse abruptly froze. Then it began to backpedal, hooves skittering on frozen ruts, until the carriage wheels slammed into a crooked fence—splinters flew. The mare's eyes rolled, foam flecking her mouth as she snorted and whinnied like something had grabbed her soul.

That's when the boy saw her.

She Wasn't Walking

A woman stood just inside the graveyard.

No, not standing. Floating.

She wore a wedding dress that shimmered like bleached skin in the moonlight—long, heavy, soaked in some dampness that refused to dry.

Her voice rasped out like snapped thread: "Oh, come on!"

And she rose. Not climbed.

Rose—as if something underneath had pushed her skyward.

She drifted toward the fence, then through it, never breaking stride. Her bare feet didn't touch the dirt road. Her veil twisted in an invisible breeze.

She stopped a few feet from the boy—smiling—but her mouth never moved. Her eyes were wet voids. She lifted a hand. Beckoning.

The horse screamed.

It reared, crashing through splintered fence posts and bolting down the icy road, the boy barely clinging to the seat as wind sliced through his jacket like knives.

The Bride Beneath the Stone

Years before, along that same road, a young woman had prepared for her wedding. The dress had been her mother's—a fragile thing stitched by hand, the color of fresh snow. As she tugged it into place, the seam tore. Her sisters scrambled for needles. Time pressed.

She was late. She panicked. Her father lashed the horses harder than he should have, and the old wagon groaned down the muddy road. The storm had left the ground churned and mean. Somewhere near a bend— where Trebein and Byron meet—the wagon hit a stone. It launched the bride skyward.

When she came down, her head met that same stone.

It split her skull like porcelain.

The gown she wore soaked red.

Her father buried her in the church cemetery just up the hill, and the groom shoved the cursed stone down into the ditch, where it still lies—choked with moss and regret.

Now She Waits

They say you can still see her—on freezing nights when the fog clings low and the moon casts everything silver.

A bride in white, dragging her ruined hem.

She's still crying out. Still screaming.

Always walking. Never getting anywhere.

And never, ever gone.

Murder in the Deep Cut
(Guernsey County)

A Road Paid in Blood

In the early 1800s, the U.S. government began carving a new path west. This road would span the wilderness and tether the young nation together. They called it the National Road. Others called it cursed. Somewhere between Old Washington and Cambridge, in a gash of earth, they hacked from the hills, workers toiled under blistering sun and black storms. Among them was one quiet man—stooped, sunburned, and stingy.

He hoarded every cent of his pay, never trusting banks, slipping his coins into stitched pockets he'd sewn into the lining of his coat. His habit was no secret.

And greed has ears.

A Butcher's Payday

One night, as mist clung low over the earth and tree limbs arched like gallows over the half-made road, he walked alone. Behind him, footfalls whispered.

They struck without a word. A shovel shattered his collarbone. A pick drove into his side. And as he begged and gurgled, they sawed off his head with a ditch blade— just so no one could name the body.

They stuffed his jingling coat beneath the loose stone that would soon become the finished roadbed. Then, they took his head and buried it elsewhere, far from the torso, somewhere unknown.

The cut was filled.

The road moved on.

But he didn't.

The Hollow That Walks

Since that night, travelers on Route 40 report a figure stumbling near the Deep Cut on fog-heavy nights—a body swaying unnaturally, dressed in threadbare work clothes soaked with old blood, its boots scraping the gravel in slow, angry drags.

It has no head. And yet it searches. Some say it stops when it senses the living—when headlights catch the glint of coins still sewn in its tattered coat. That's when it listens.

That's when it turns—though there's no neck to pivot, no eyes to see.

Just the cold, wet scrape of bone on stone and the faint sound of gurgling breath that never finished dying.

And it still digs.

With broken fingers. With stumps. With will alone.

Because its skull is still out there, somewhere in the black earth of eastern Ohio.

And until the murdered man can fit his head to his spine and close his own grave—He walks.

And waits.

The Singer, the Shadow, the Screaming, and the Ghost
(Hamilton County)

A Road That Should've Grown Quiet

About five miles from Carthage, a narrow dirt road once slipped down through a winding hollow, fenced in by thick woods and a thin, black stream. Even in summer, the fog clung to the trees like breath on cold glass.

Horses balked. Wheels skidded.

And travelers—if they had any sense—avoided it altogether. But those who passed through swore they heard it: A strange voice, drunken and singsong, rising from the brush.

There is old Sam Simons

And young Sam Simons

Who is old Sam Simons' son..

The voice was so close you could almost touch it. But no one ever saw a soul.

The Singer, the Shadow, and the Screaming

One night, a drunk man walking the hollow heard the song and sang along. The voice stopped. A woman's voice answered—soft at first, almost gentle. A man responded. But the words soon sharpened, brittle, and cracked until their argument splintered into a rage.

Then, a man's scream tore the silence: "Oh, my God!"

From the underbrush, a small, crooked shadow burst out and vanished into the trees. That road has never truly known peace since.

The Sisters on the Hill

Long ago, two half-sisters—Ellen Doll and Mary Riddell—lived alone in a farmhouse atop the hill where the road curled out of the hollow. After their parents died in 1845, the girls managed the farm with the assistance of an aging hired hand. But when he passed, they hired a new hand: a handsome drifter named Andy Maginnis.

He sang, played the fiddle, worked hard, danced well, and wore clean shirts when he called on the sisters. Everyone said he had an eye for both.

Love, Jealousy, and Death

In November of 1847, a farmer hauling grain found two corpses just off the old road. One was Mary—bruised, strangled, and cold. A dagger sat in her hand. The other was a middle-aged man face-down in the mud, reeking of liquor and blood. When they rushed to the house, they found Ellen dazed, bleeding from the head. She said they'd been attacked and that she'd passed out. That she didn't know Mary had died until they told her of the tragic death. Ellen wept and appeared inconsolable. One man brought the dagger to her and showed her the weapon used to kill their assailant, and Ellen recognized it immediately as her father's old blade. She admitted that the two women would carry it for protection. No one questioned the tale. No one wanted to.

The Dagger and the Lie

Andy vanished. Ellen sold the farm and moved to Cincinnati. Years later, wracked with fever, she made a deathbed confession to a nurse: "I killed my sister. And I also killed the man beside her. I did not plan on doing it, though," she whispered hoarsely to the nurse who attended her and was particularly aware she was listening to Ellen's dying words. "My half-sister and I attended the singing school that night and returned home unescorted. As we walked, we both admitted to being in love with Andy Maginnis, which hurt my heart. I told her she must give him up because I loved him more. She said it did not matter because she must marry him to save our good name. She was having his baby. I lost my head then, for it was the same reason I must marry him.

I reached out, grabbed her by the neck, and began to throttle her. Then she suddenly fell to the ground dead." Ellen had taken in raspy breaths, then continued. "It was then I heard drunken singing—

There is old Sam Simons

And young Sam Simons

Who is old Sam Simons' son..

Not a moment later, it stopped, and I felt a hand upon my shoulder. Startled, I saw a bedraggled and inebriated man behind me. The wretch told me he saw me kill her, and if I did not do what he demanded, he would kill me too. But I had my father's old dagger on me when he threw me to the ground, and I stabbed him mercilessly until he lay dead." Ellen's voice trailed off, and she died.

And the hollow never slept again.

Where the Asphalt Doesn't Reach

The house rotted. The road crumbled. The woods took over—until developers buried the stream and paved over the hollow with sidewalks, streetlights, and new homes. But some nights, beneath the hum of passing cars, the song still rises from the grass.

There is old Sam Simons

And young Sam Simons

Who is old Sam Simons' son...

Then the whispering starts. Then the scream. And if you walk that stretch after dark, you may glimpse Ellen in a blur of white darting from the trees. Not a girl. Not anymore. Just a wraith—trapped in that last, wretched second of wickedness. Still running from her guilt.

Headless Conductor of Weidler's Pass
(Hancock County)

In the bitter chill of November 1889, the wind scoured the flat farmland outside Findlay, screaming between fence rails and rattling the skeleton trees near B. Weidler's property. A short bypass siding split off from the Lake Erie and Western Railroad—a temporary detour for freight cars to wait while others thundered past. That day, conductor Jimmy Welsh rode the rear of a freight train, making its routine run toward Fostoria.

But the routine ended in violence.

Just past a lonely road crossing, the couplings gave. A car disconnected, swaying violently before flinging Welsh down between the rails. He hit the gravel hard—but had no time to scream. The rear half of the train, unaware of the break, came screaming behind him.

And crushed him.

His body was mangled instantly. The steel wheels sheared his head clean from his shoulders, grinding it into the frozen ballast. Blood painted the stones. Bones jutted like snapped corn stalks. His lantern—a brass thing he always carried—was found two hundred feet down the line, still lit, glowing pale, and useless in the cold.

The Ghost With No Face

It didn't take long for stories to spread.

By January, just weeks after Jimmy's death, train crews running the midnight shift between Findlay and Fostoria reported an eerie sight. At the precise place where Welsh had died, a lantern now danced in the darkness—swinging slowly at first, then whipping violently from side to side as if gripped by invisible hands. Behind it—a headless man staggered along the rails. His neck was jagged and black, still oozing what looked like shadow instead of blood. His coat was torn and stiff with frost, and his feet moved with mechanical jerks like a puppet on broken strings. Always searching for his head. The first time a fireman saw it, he leapt from the moving engine in terror and never returned to rail work again.

Still Out There

They say you can still see him—especially in November—when the fog hangs low to the ground, and the wind smells faintly of rust and soil. The lantern appears first. Then, the outline of the figure. If you're unlucky, he'll pause and slowly turn as if he can still see you—even without eyes.

If he steps toward you, don't wait.

Because Jimmy Welsh wants his head back.

And maybe yours will do.

The Marsh That Should Have Stayed Wet
(Hardin County)

Before the fields and furrows, Hog Creek Marsh once sprawled between Ada and Dola, Ohio—a shallow lake tangled in wild grasses and cranberries, its still waters brimming with small creatures that skittered, croaked, and thrived. But in 1868, the marsh was dredged, its life drained out for crops. Men with boots and shovels turned it into farmland, thinking they'd claimed something from the earth. They were wrong.

The Tap-Tap-Tap of Forgotten Things

Old folks in Dola tell it quietly, like a prayer they'd rather not speak. Each year, after the harvest is stored and the chill of October sets in, the animals come back. Not living—but watching. The air thickens near the edges of the fields. That's when the tapping starts. Soft at first. Then sharper. Tap. Tap. Tap.

Tiny nails on farmhouse windows.

Their eyes glow in the dark—too low to the ground to be human, too wide to be anything natural. Shapes dart between cornrows. Shadows linger by the silos. And sometimes, in the middle of the night, the dogs won't bark. They only whine and hide.

The Riders Return

And then there are the riders. At midnight on Halloween, some say you can hear hooves on wet earth, though there's no swamp left to soak them. The Wyandot come riding along the phantom shoreline, just as they did before they were forced from their lands in July of 1843. They make no sound save for the whisper of their passing—no war cry.

No warning. Just motion.

They vanish into the corn, where tall shocks appear by morning—neatly stacked, towering, and not made by any hand in Dola. No one claims them. No one dares knock them down. Because this was theirs and still is.

Searching for His Blade
(Harrison County)

The Soldier Stands

Atop a hill in Dickerson Cemetery, the soldier's statue doesn't sleep. By day, it stands silent—its rust-streaked sword broken, its stone chipped with age. But after dark, they say its neck groans in a slow, splintering twist. It's looking for the one who broke its blade.

Bill Bellington Still Works the Buckland's Lock

(Henry County)

Where the Miami and Erie Canal met the Maumee River near Providence, Ohio, boatmen used to pass through a series of locks on the slack water fed by the Providence Dam. One of those was Buckland's Lock, a guard lock that let boats from the Gilead Canal across the river connect into the Erie system.

In the 1800s, crews working this route reported something strange.

As they neared Buckland's Lock at night, they heard what sounded like groans from the brush near the waterline. Some described it as a man in pain. Others said it sounded more like muttering—low and rasping.

Then, fog would settle along the canal.

And a man would appear in the mist.

Small. Stooped. Thin. He would shuffle toward the sluice gate as if working it. The lock would open. Barges drifted forward. But once inside, the gate would close again—no one visible, no one there.

It kept happening. Lock after lock.

Same man. Same fog.

Always just before midnight.

The Lock Keeper's Death

The last official keeper at Buckland's Lock was William Bellington. Locals called him Bill.

He lived in a single-room shanty across the road from the canal. Bill drank most of the day and was rarely seen without a bottle in hand. In the 1880s, a fire broke out in the shanty near midnight. By the time help came, the structure had already collapsed.

In the morning, Bellington's body was found burned inside. Charred black.

There were rumors.

He'd kept his canal pay hidden in the house—silver coins tucked under the stove in a tin. The tin was never found. The fire was ruled an accident, but locals didn't believe it. There was no lamp oil spilled. No cause was ever given. He died alone. And possibly not by chance.

After the Fire

The strange lock incidents began shortly after.

Boatmen on night runs swore they saw a man working the gears. The description always matched Bellington. Same size. Same walk.

No one ever saw his face.

Sometimes, the locks moved on their own. Other times, the figure was seen ahead, disappearing each time the boats reached the gate. The iron windlass would spin. The gates would swing open. And then close again—loud, sudden, without warning.

The fog would thicken.

And no one would speak until they were through the last gate.

What's Left

The canal is dry now. The shanty is gone. But those who walk the path at dusk say it's not quiet.

Some nights, the metal hardware around Buckland's Lock groans like it's still being turned. A burnt smell lingers across the water when there's no fire.

And near the old shanty's footprint, where nothing grows—footsteps are heard.

Walking. Circling. Waiting. Bill Bellington is still working the Buckland's Lock.

Capering Imp of Dunn's Chapel
(Highland County)

A farmer was heading west along Anderson Road on August 30, 1888 just before midnight. He'd passed Dunn's Chapel and the small cemetery behind it when he heard something low and rough to his right. It wasn't a voice. It sounded like a snarl dragged through gravel. He stopped the wagon. Looked toward the stones. A white figure moved between them—too large for a rabbit, too smooth for a man. Thinking it was a dog or calf, he whistled. The thing turned and growled.

It Cleared the Fence

The creature leapt the iron fence in one bound. Its limbs hit the ground wrong—too long in front, hunched behind. White fur covered its back and what looked like wings stretched out from its shoulders.

It circled him in the grass. Fast, low to the earth. The farmer didn't move.

He described it later as having a head and chest far larger than its back end. Its legs were uneven. Its body narrowed down to a tail that flicked behind it like a whip.

It wasn't flying.

It walked.

But the wings moved.

He Pulled His Knife

Still frozen, he reached slowly into his coat and pulled out a pocket knife. Took one step. Then another.

The thing crouched. Its tail snapped back and forth. Its wings rose slightly, then lowered again. The eyes flared yellow in the dark. The teeth were visible—long, sharp, and white.

It didn't rush him. It waited.

The Bridge

He kept moving, one foot at a time, until he reached the bridge at the edge of the chapel property. That's when it blocked the path.

It stopped on its haunches, staring. The farmer said it looked like it could leap straight through him.

Then something changed. Dogs started barking from a neighbor's farm—loud, insistent.

The creature turned sharply and bolted into the woods, disappearing without sound.

The trees swallowed it.

What He Found in the Morning

The farmer came back at dawn. He didn't sleep.

On one grave, he found long rake marks in the dirt. On the road were fresh prints—three toes each, with a long central claw. Not from a dog or deer.

They looked like a bird's.

But oversized.

Like a chicken, but wrong.

No Explanation

No other sightings were reported that week. No animals went missing. No bodies turned up.

Only the grave scratches remained.

And the tracks.

The Baying Hound of Old Man's Cave

(Hocking County)

Visitors walking near Upper Falls have reported the sound of a hound dog deep in the gorge. It doesn't echo from the top. It comes from down in the stone belly of the cave. The sound rises slowly. Then it starts to move.

People follow it—past the waterfall, down the long stairway, and onto the trail that follows the stream. The path bends, narrows, and runs beneath a vast recess cave.

That's where the howling grows sharpest.

And then it stops.

Just air and running water.

No dog. No trace.

The Boys Who Found Him

Around 1870, two boys from South Bloomingville followed the same sound. They'd heard stories about the gorge. Some said it was haunted. Others said a ghost dog patrolled the creek beds after dark.

The boys climbed into a shallow cave cut into the rock. That's when they saw him.

An old man with a gray beard. A large white dog followed at his side. The man wore buckskins and carried a long rifle. He walked toward the edge of the cave—then vanished into the ground. They ran home.

The Grave in the Stone

Neighbors came back the next day with tools. At the dip in the rock where the man disappeared, they dug.

They uncovered two skeletons. One man. One dog.

They also found an old flintlock rifle and a few blackened cooking pots. Carved into the rock nearby was a name: *Retzler*. And the year: *1777*.

Forgotten Bones

Tourists once came to see the grave. They stood near the carved stone and pointed at the bones. But eventually, the remains were buried elsewhere, and the marker faded.

People stopped coming.

And the dog was forgotten.

The Trapper

Long before Logan or Cedar Grove were settled, trappers lived rough along Cedar Creek. Retzler was one of them. He and his dog, Harper, took shelter in the gorge over winter.

When neighbors realized Retzler hadn't been seen, they followed his path—grown over and quiet.

They found the man and the dog both dead inside the cave. No wounds. No signs of a fight. Just still.

They buried them there.

What Comes After

The sound still returns. Not often. But always at night.

One autumn, a park ranger on evening patrol heard a dog howling below the falls. He thought it was a lost hiker's pet or someone poaching in the park.

He followed the trail, flashlight in hand. The howl moved with him, echoing down the walls. It stopped near the old rock shelf above the water.

He scanned the trees. Nothing moved. There was only cold stone surrounding him. And silence.

The Story They Told

Old men in South Bloomingville used to say Retzler's dog never left. They said Harper bayed so loud the night his master died that it shook the leaves from the trees.

Now he just waits. And sometimes—he calls.

Ash Cave: Thirteen on the Trail
(Hocking County)

It was early spring when Pat Quackenbush, a longtime park naturalist, led a small group of twelve hikers on a guided night walk to Ash Cave at Hocking Hills State Park. Nothing spooky. No ghost talk.

Just nature, sandstone cliffs, and whatever the forest decided to offer. The hike was a short half-mile along a concrete walkway to a large recess in the sandstone known as Ash Cave, where a waterfall cascades down a cliff.

Twelve Hikers

There were twelve people in this small group, and as they walked, Pat would frequently pause beneath the hemlocks and cliffs to face the group, pointing out unique features along the trail. He particularly enjoyed sharing his famous personal story about the ghostly lights that hikers would see along the trail at dusk.

His absolute favorite?

Pat discovered that the ghostly lights hikers would see along the trail at dusk were actually caused by flying squirrels that had rolled in bioluminescent fungus, making them glow like lightning bugs! (And now that Pat is retired, the story of the glowing flying squirrels remains one of his most memorable discoveries and one that only he could deliver with a straight face—a truly unique tale that belongs to him alone.)

But each time they stopped, he silently counted the hikers to ensure that everyone was accounted for. He did not want anyone getting lost in the dark! "...ten, eleven, twelve..." Once Pat confirmed that he had everyone, he pointed out a deer that was almost hidden in the grass. He imitated the call of a barred owl, which was soon answered by a couple of hoots from deep within the forest that held the tune, "Who cooks for *youuuu allll*?"

Pat always took a moment before each stop, as there were often one or two stragglers who would become captivated by the enchanting trail. "...ten, eleven..." he counted in his head. "Yep—twelve. All here." He patiently waited for anyone trailing behind to catch up before sharing interesting facts about the unique area.

No, Thirteen Hikers

About a quarter of the way into the hike, Pat noticed that one hiker had emerged from the shadows just as he began his talk.

"...ten, eleven, twelve—and," he counted again. "Hmm, thirteen?"

Initially, Pat thought he might have miscounted the group, but he dismissed the idea. Perhaps this extra hiker had wanted to enjoy the walk alone under the immense hemlocks, which was not as concerning as having one fewer person in the group.

So, instead of pausing to recount everyone, Pat decided to continue, believing the straggler would eventually catch up.

When he reached the halfway point, he stopped to discuss an ancient beech tree near the trail. The group formed a half-circle around him, and while they did, he quickly counted everyone once more. "...ten, eleven, twelve..."

He looked up and noticed that the straggler was only about five feet away from the other hikers.

"Thirteen!" He had counted correctly! However, number thirteen was unlike the rest. He observed that she was dressed in old-fashioned clothing—a feed sack dress typically worn by thrifty women during the 19th-century Great Depression who used flour and feed sacks to make their dresses.

The mysterious guest seemed so out of place that it caught him off guard, prompting him to bring it to the group's attention.

"I turned my attention behind the group," Pat recounted, "and asked if they could see the woman who was standing there and had been following us. I watched them reluctantly turn around, and there were more than a few gasps. I wasn't alone—everyone on that hike saw her." Then, she took two steps and vanished into the woods.

She Still Walks the Trail

Since that encounter, others have noticed the lone hiker who lingers behind the group. Occasionally, witnesses have reported seeing a woman peeking from behind a tree before disappearing.

Salem Cemetery Angel of Death
(Holmes County)

Just outside the quiet farm community of Saltillo, the Salem Reformed Church once stood on a hilltop. It's gone now—torn down after the war when the last of the congregation scattered. But the cemetery remains. And so does the angel. Among the headstones stands a monument taller than the rest. Fifteen feet high and carved in stone. A five-foot angel stood at its peak, hands folded, head bowed.

The Grave of Mary Conrad

In April 1890, Mary Conrad died at the age of fifty-seven. Her husband George, a prosperous farmer who owned land just south of the cemetery, buried her beneath a towering monument—fifteen feet tall, crowned with a five-foot angel. Years later, George was laid beside her.

The angel still stands. But she's not the same.

The Headless Watcher

By the 1920s, stories began to spread—first whispered in schoolyards, then passed around in Sunday quiet.

People said the angel moved. They said her head turned.

If you looked into her face at midnight, you wouldn't last the week. Some called it a legend. Others said it was true because they knew someone—always someone else—who had died not long after daring the gaze.

Her stare, they claimed, was death itself.

A Game for the Brave

Teenagers turned it into a test. At night, they'd drive out to the cemetery with flashlights and beer, daring each other to stand in front of the statue. Some swore they saw the head shift. One boy fainted. Another girl screamed and ran, swearing she heard the angel whisper her name.

Most made it home. Not all.

What's Missing

She's headless now. Her wings are broken.

Her arms shattered at the elbows.

Vandals tried to destroy her. The head was stolen more than once—dragged away and later returned, sometimes left sitting upright beside the base.

But she remembers.

The Car Wreck

One year, not long ago, a boy took her head. He didn't make it home. His car went off the road in the rain, flipping twice before striking a tree. Police arrived at the scene and found the trunk bent inward. Inside, they found the angel's head.

The boy's skull was split in the same place as the statue's damage. They buried him closed-casket.

After that, trustees took the head and hid it where no one would find it again.

After Midnight

She doesn't need it. The statue still stands at the edge of the trees. And sometimes, on cold nights when the sky is dark, a faint flicker moves along the hilltop. It moves like wings—but broken ones.

Some say she lifts from the base and glides across the grass. Others have seen nothing—but woke with nosebleeds and bruises after walking too close.

Light bothers her. So she finds it. And when she does— she moves.

Haunting at the Old Blue Bridge
(Huron County)

During the War of 1812, a blockhouse stood near Milan to shield settlers from attack. It was built fast, rough, and held together with desperation. The land beyond it was still contested.

Two boys left it one morning—young and armed with little more than axes and a reason.

They were after a bee tree.

The Killing

Samuel Seymour was eighteen. Reuben Pixley, Jr. was fifteen. They followed a small stream south from the fort until it joined with the West Branch of the Huron River. They found the tree along the bank and started their work—chopping, scraping, pulling out wax and honey.

They never saw who fired. Seymour was hit clean through and fell without a sound. Pixley tried to run but caught his leg in the underbrush. They took him. He was held captive for months. Samuel was left behind. His body stayed where it dropped.

The Haunting at the Fork

The stream where the incident occurred was later named Seymour Creek. It still meets the West Branch in a narrow valley just off Lamereaux Road.

Long after the war, people began reporting strange occurrences near the crossing, which they referred to as the Old Blue Bridge. Lights in the trees. Mist curling up from dry earth. Even in the heat of summer, fog rolled up from the banks where Seymour died. Some said the lights moved as if someone were carrying them—up the hillside, across the water. Others swore they saw the shadow of a man standing by the brush line. Not moving.

Just watching.

What Remains

There's no fort now. No bee tree. But Seymour Creek still runs, shallow and brown, behind the timber and thorns. On some nights, the water glows faintly in the hollow. And the lights return.

He never made it back. And he never left that spot.

The Ghost of Salem Cemetery Road

(Jackson County)

Berlin Crossroads was settled in the early 1800s by African Americans—some freeborn, some newly freed. It grew into a quiet farming community and a trusted link on the route to freedom. Those escaping from Kentucky and Virginia passed through the town. They came through the woods at night and followed footpaths to the farm of Noah Nooks. He guided them toward Wilkesville, Albany, and Athens. Some made it. Some didn't.

The Woman Beside the Road

Years later, long after the war, local folks traveling by buggy near the Old Baptist Cemetery began seeing something strange. Just as they passed the stone markers along Salem Cemetery Road, a woman would appear. She walked beside the road in a long white robe. Not running. Just moving. Quickly. She matched the speed of the carriage, even uphill. Most assumed she was headed for the Crossroads—someone out late, maybe returning to family. But when they glanced down at her face, the illusion fell apart. Her skin was gray. Her mouth hung open, slack and silent. And her eyes didn't blink.

Who She Was

No one could say. She never spoke.

But people knew the land had kept secrets. Most outsiders never asked questions about the comings and goings at Berlin Crossroads. They knew enough to look away. It's believed she was one of those who never made it. Maybe she died crossing the river. Maybe she was caught before she reached the Nooks farm. Or maybe she made it to the edge of safety—and collapsed just before the door opened.

Still Moving

They still see her. Even now, drivers on Salem Cemetery Road report a flash of white beside the ditch line. Some say they catch her just out of the corner of their eye—moving fast, head down, walking against the dark. Always walking. Never arriving. Her path runs between two worlds—freedom and death.

And she belongs to neither.

Ghost at a Boarding House
(Jefferson County)

At a boarding house in McCoy's station near Steubenville in early June of 1886, the fight started late Sunday night and dragged into Monday morning. No one heard exactly what was said through the thin walls of the room; it was muffled. Edward Householder, 32, and his mistress, Nancy Mushrush Weire, 38, had shared a boarding room for several months. Neighbors heard them fighting often. This night was no different. She was angry. He was drunk.

The Murder

By Tuesday evening, Nancy Weire was dead. Her throat had been cut clean across. There were several stab wounds to the chest. She was found on the floor of the boarding house room—

The Steubenville Herald reported:

"At 6 o'clock this evening, Nancy Weire, a woman aged about 38, was found dead at McCoy's Station in this county, with her throat cut from ear to ear and several stab wounds on her breast. She had a penknife in her hand. It is not known whether this is a case of suicide or murder, but the general belief is that she was murdered and the knife subsequently placed in her hand."

Witnesses later testified that Edward had been seen wearing a blue flannel shirt the day before. That shirt, soaked in blood, was found stuffed behind a trunk in the room. A knife belonging to Edward was recovered beside the body.

There was blood on his clothing when they arrested him. He said he didn't remember doing it. He blamed "bad women."

He blamed whiskey. The jury did not.

Her Past

Nancy Weire was no stranger to violent men. In 1867, nearly twenty years earlier, she had been involved in another killing. On April 6 of that year, Lewis K. McCoy— Nancy's then-lover—shot and killed Joseph McDonald during a dispute at the train station. Some believed Nancy helped lure McDonald there.

Others claimed she watched it happen.

McCoy was sentenced to life in prison after spending over $100,000 on his defense. He was pardoned in 1870 and lived out the rest of his days quietly. Nancy did not.

The Ghost at the Boarding House

After Nancy was buried in Toronto Union Cemetery, her room didn't stay empty for long. But those who took it didn't stay either. Tenants began complaining of strange cold drafts and the feeling of being watched. At night, the doorknob would rattle. Lamps flickered.

Then came the first sighting.

The Stranger Who Didn't Know

Ashbrook was a drummer—a traveling salesman passing through town. He hadn't meant to stop at McCoy's Station but was forced to stay when the Ohio River was too dangerous to cross due to heavy ice. The hotel was fully booked, so he was directed to a boarding house. He ended up in the room that no one ever wanted to stay in. He accepted it, perhaps not knowing or caring, as it was the only one available in town.

That night, he left the lamp on and went to bed.

What happened next was printed in the local paper:

"He said a dread feeling came over him around midnight, as though another person was in the room. He opened his eyes and looked in the direction of the lamp, where he saw a rather attractive woman sitting in a chair, wearing a man's white hat and a brown calico dress. Ashbrook asked what she wanted but received no reply. He then got up and approached the woman, but just as he was about to lay a hand upon her, the apparition vanished, and the lamp went out."

Ashbrook told the story the next morning, thinking it was a strange dream. But others knew better.

He had described exactly what Nancy wore the day she died.

He had never heard of her.

She Never Left

The boarding house changed hands often, but the stories never stopped.

Those who stayed in the upstairs room spoke in whispers. The chair by the lamp scraped across the floor at night—slow, deliberate. A man's white hat appeared on the hallway hook, then vanished before morning.

The blood never left the floorboards.

They tried sanding. Scrubbing.

Covered it with a rug.

It came back.

Tenants heard crying after midnight. Not loud. Just beneath the breath—like someone kneeling in the corner, choking back sound.

Some woke to find the mirror fogged over. No heat in the room. No closed windows. It was just a breath pattern drawn on glass that wasn't theirs.

The doorknob would click once and stop. Never open.

As if someone had come in.

And stayed.

Few lasted more than a week.

And those who did…said they saw her shadow move across the foot of the bed. Even when the room was empty.

Miranda Still Walks to Maplehurst Mansion
(Knox County)

It was the Saturday night before Easter. Miranda Bricker had finished visiting her sister and was headed back to the place she worked—Maplehurst Mansion, the grand home of the Fairchild family. It sat at the corner of Division and East Gambier streets in Mount Vernon.

Miranda, 56 years old, had worked as a maid there since the previous October. One of the house's benefits was a small room she used on the second floor.

She was tired. Wanted to retire early.

It was after 9:00 p.m.

Cool. Cloudy. Quiet.

She stepped from Division Street onto the gravel path.

That was as far as she got.

The Killing

Something hit her face—hard.

The blow was so strong it knocked the dentures straight from her mouth. She screamed once: "Oh, my God!"

A neighbor, Mrs. Swigert, heard it. She stepped out and looked toward the yard. There were shapes moving in the grass. She heard a gurgling sound. She assumed it was drunks off the train.

Didn't go closer.

The next morning, one of the Fairchild maids opened the curtain and looked out over the lawn.

Miranda was lying dead in the grass.

The Search

Police brought in bloodhounds. The dogs followed a scent trail that led through alleys, across a field, and finally stopped near a quarry and the home of a man named George Copeland.

He was arrested on the spot. The crowd gathered fast—talk of a lynching spread before noon. But Copeland denied everything. There were no witnesses. No murder weapon. No evidence. They had to let him go.

No one else was ever charged.

No one else was ever found.

She Still Walks

For years, people on Division Street claimed to see her—a woman in servant's dress walking the gravel path toward the Fairchild door, just as she had the night she was killed.

But her figure never reached the mansion.

She always stopped in the grass.

Turned once.

And disappeared.

The Stain That Stayed

The housemaids wouldn't walk that yard after dark. One claimed she found the impression of a body in the grass two years after the murder. Another heard the faint crack of gravel and a voice rasp, "Oh, my God," though no one was nearby.

The house changed hands. The path wore down. But the stories remained even after the old place was torn down.

A blow took her down. And no one ever paid for it.

Now she walks the same route—never reaching the door.

The Body in the Wall at Fairport Harbor Lighthouse
(Lake County)

The Fairport Harbor Lighthouse once guided ships through the dark chop of Lake Erie. It was a point of safety. But for those who stayed inside its walls, it became something else entirely. A place where things never quite left. In the 1800s, the lighthouse wasn't just a station for sailors. It served another purpose—quiet, hidden.

Runaways fleeing slavery passed through its back rooms and headed north to Canada. There are no formal records. Just names whispered.

The lighthouse kept secrets.

Some still breathe through the brick.

Keeper Babcock

In 1871, Captain Joseph Babcock took over as keeper. He moved his wife and children into the tower's small residence. They brought with them a handful of cats.

People remembered the cats. Always watching from windowsills. Always just underfoot.

Years passed. The family left. But not all of them.

The Thing Behind the Wall

Long after the light had gone cold, the tower became a museum. Volunteers came in to preserve it—dusting corners and replacing fixtures. During the installation of an air conditioning system, workers opened a wall near the old living quarters. Inside, they found it.

A cat.

Dried and mummified, its body curled in a crawl space behind the plaster. No one could say how long it had been there. But the claws were still drawn. The mouth was slightly open.

What Came After

The sightings had started before the discovery.

Volunteers reported hearing something small move through the rooms. Nails tapping on hardwood. A shadow slipped under a table. Some swore they saw the cat itself—faint, pale, but fast.

It darted from room to room, always just out of reach. When followed, it vanished through the walls. And sometimes, when the building was locked up at night, the alarm system triggered.

The Cat and the Lighthouse

The Fairport Harbor Lighthouse still stands, watching the lake. It's clean, restored, and open to the public.

But not everything inside is part of the tour.

Visitors say the ghost cat still flits through the rooms—fluffy, faint, and fast. A soft blur at the edge of sight. It never knocks anything over. It just appears, turns once, and slips into the wall like smoke.

Some swear they hear it purring behind the plaster.

And if it likes you, it might meow when you start to leave a room.

Or better or worse—depending on how you feel about cats and ghosts—follow you into the next one.

The Man in White on the Tracks
(Lawrence County)

The old depot is long gone in Ironton, but the stories haven't left.

Where the double-track spur once ran near Front and Second Streets, people used to speak carefully—sometimes only after dark—about the things they saw near the rails. Things they couldn't quite explain.

A figure. Pale, unnatural. A presence that felt wrong.

The Night It Appeared

Frank Brown, a clerk at the corner grocery, was walking home one evening when he was stopped by his neighbors, Mr. and Mrs. Winkle. They lived near Buckhorn Street and looked visibly shaken. Both were pale, their voices unsteady.

They told him they'd just seen something out back. Something white and slow-moving drifting across the rail line behind their house. It had turned toward them—face visible, though they didn't want to describe it.

Terrified, the couple fled inside. But Frank, more curious than afraid, decided to go take a look.

The Man in White

He followed the path toward the tracks. The ground was damp from an earlier rain, the gravel dark and slick. For a moment, everything seemed still—quiet, empty.

Then, out of the mist, a figure began to take shape.

A man in a white suit stood just beyond the rail line. His head was bowed. His arms hung loosely at his sides. There was no movement, no sound.

Frank took a few cautious steps forward. In an instant, the figure vanished—dissolving into the fog like it had never been there at all.

The Story Behind It

It wasn't the first time someone had seen that figure. Years earlier, a man had come to Portsmouth from West Virginia with his wife and children. He'd been waiting near the depot for a train. Some said he was exhausted. Others whispered he might have been drunk.

Either way, at some point, he lay down across the tracks. His family remained seated on a bench nearby, unaware of what he'd done. When the freight train rolled through, it was already too late.

The wheels didn't stop.

They rarely ever do.

What Remained

The railroad men who found the body never told the whole story. Just fragments—enough to unsettle anyone who heard them.

They said the man had been wearing a blue suit when he arrived.

By the time they pulled him from the rails, it had turned white.

His head was discovered six yards down the track. His arms had been caught and torn by the wheels. The rest of him was barely recognizable—what was left had to be removed with shovels.

What Still Walks

Now, on certain fog-heavy nights, when the air hangs low over the place where the old spur once crossed the street, some say you can still see him.

Not moving quickly. Not crying out.

Just walking that same short path between Front and Second, dressed in a suit that only looks white when the light hits it wrong. And sometimes, when the wind dies and the night goes still, you can hear it—the slow, grating hiss of iron dragging over bone.

Still Haunting the Cells of Licking County Jail
(Licking County)

Built in 1889, the Licking County Jail was never meant to be merciful. It held murderers, madmen, and monsters. One of them was Missus Laura Belle Devlin— better known as the Handsaw Slayer. On January 6th, 1947, she carved up her 72-year-old husband with a sickle and saw. She fed his limbs into the coal stove, piece by piece until there was nothing left but ash and the stench of cooked flesh.

The Dead Within

Inside those stone walls, at least twenty-two people died. Seven took their own lives. Four were sheriffs who dropped dead from heart attacks, one after another. And one... was torn from his cell and lynched in the street.

In 1910, Newark had more than 80 saloons and 30 brothels. Prohibitionists were furious. The Ohio Anti-Saloon League sent in private detectives to clean up the city. One of them was a 17-year-old redhead from Kentucky—Carl Etherington.

On July 8th, Etherington shot saloon owner William Howard during a botched raid. The locals didn't care that Howard had started it. They caught Etherington, beat him bloody, and dragged him to a cell in the jail.

That night, a mob smashed through the steel door using a rail tie. As the terrified boy sobbed to a guard— "What will mother say when she hears of this?"—they pulled him from the cell and beat him again. Some say he died there, on the floor. Others say they strung him up, still breathing. They dragged him into the street and hanged him from a telegraph pole while thousands watched—cheering, laughing. Children were there, too. The aftermath led to murder indictments, a fired sheriff, and a mayor's resignation. But some things couldn't be erased. Today, doors slam with no wind. Cries echo down empty corridors. Footsteps pace where no feet walk. Some say Carl Etherington still weeps in his cell. Others claim the Handsaw Slayer paces near the old stove, looking for her next piece. You don't have to believe it.

You can go see for yourself.

The Hatchet Man of Township Highway 56

(Logan County)

Andrew Hellman arrived from Germany in 1817, a tailor by trade with a charming smile and a reputation for good manners. He married Mary Abel—a cheerful, lively woman—and together, they built a modest farm outside Huntsville along what is now Township Highway 56. To neighbors, they seemed the picture of early frontier success. Three children, a growing homestead, and the promise of peace.

But something darker lived inside Andrew. Something no one saw—until it was far too late.

April 1839

One morning, Mary awoke to the sound of retching.

Her daughter Louisa, 17, and her youngest son John, only 12, had grown deathly ill overnight. Their skin turned gray, their eyes sunken, and their breath reeked of rot. Within hours, both children were dead. A third child, Henry, who was 16 years old, barely survived.

They were buried in a single grave before the week's end. No doctor could say for sure what took them—only that it came fast and left Mary a mother of one.

It was afterward, as Mary stood at the table and lifted the milk jug, that she noticed the powder. Clinging to the rim. Unsifted. Undissolved. She did not drink it.

She said nothing to her husband. Only whispered her fear in a letter to her sister, a line scrawled in shaky ink: "I do not think they died natural."

The Silence that Followed

The truth was too terrible to face—too monstrous to believe. But Mary had lived it. In small ways. In bruises. On long nights. In the fear that kept her from speaking.

She sent Henry to live with her brother George. A week passed. Then another. No one heard from her again.

George's wife came looking. She stepped into the house and dropped to her knees, screaming.

Mary was sprawled across the floor, butchered. The ax was still embedded in her skull. Blood soaked the bedding where Andrew had calmly laid beside her corpse.

Escape and Second Slaughter

Jailed and questioned, Andrew Hellman vanished before justice could be served. He fled to Maryland, changed his name to Adam Horn, and started anew like the past was nothing more than a shirt he had taken off.

There, he married again—a girl of just sixteen named Malinda. By 1843, her body was found in pieces: limbs stuffed in burlap coffee sacks, her torso jammed into a trunk in the loft. The house smelled of mold and decay for weeks before her remains were uncovered.

This time, he did not escape.

The crowd at his hanging was massive—nearly a thousand gathered to watch the Hatchet Man swing. They said he never wept. Never begged. Just stared coldly into the crowd like he knew he'd return.

The Road Where He Waits

Today, they say Andrew Hellman never left Township Highway 56. On cold nights, especially in March, drivers see a man along the roadside—gaunt, with hollow eyes and a hatchet clenched in one fist.

So, if you find yourself alone on Township Highway 56 after dark, and you see him—don't stop.

Don't slow down. Don't meet his eyes.

Because he's still smiling—too wide, too knowing—like he already picked you. And sometimes, even when you don't stop, you hear the back door click shut.

You feel the weight behind you. You smell old blood and wet earth. By then, it's already too late.

The Ghost of Cottesbrooke Curve
(Lorain County)

It was a sweltering Sunday evening in Elyria in the summer of 1903—July 16, and 6:30 p.m. to the minute—when steel and speed met death just southwest of Elyria.

Two interurban electric cars, one eastbound from Oberlin, the other westbound from Elyria, barreled toward each other on the same track. A misunderstanding of orders. A delay at the Lowry switch. A curve too sharp to see past. No time to brake.

As one car reached the Black River Bridge, the other emerged from around the bend at Cottesbrooke Curve.

The collision was described in The Elyria Chronicle as one of the worst in memory:

"E.L. Garvin, a well-known printer of Oberlin... was instantly killed, his neck being broken and his legs badly crushed."

Car No. 99, a newly serviced steel-wrapped behemoth, plowed through the older wooden Car No. 67, slicing it nearly in half—telescoping the passenger cabin like a blade into soft flesh. Bones broke. Flesh tore. Glass sprayed through the air like shrapnel. Screams filled the ravine. And then—only silence.

The Haunting Begins

It wasn't long after the blood was scrubbed from the track that the stories began. That December, a trolley motorman neared Cottesbrooke Curve in the dark when he saw someone standing on the rails. A shadow. Still and waiting. He sounded his whistle. Slowed to a crawl.

But the figure vanished the moment his headlight struck it. Night after night, it returned, always in the same place. Always gone by the time light reached it.

A Crash That Never Came—But Was Heard

Later that winter, two section men were dispatched to clear snow at the site of the wreck. As they worked, they heard it: the approach of a trolley car. *"Nearer and nearer it came... until its deafening noise was upon them,"* the Wooster Weekly Republican reported. *"But no car was to be seen. No headlight broke the gloom."* Then—a terrible crash. Not the whistle or rattle of a passing car.

But there was the sound of splintered iron and death, as if two trains had collided just beside them. And in the stillness that followed: *"A cry, of a human being in mortal anguish… then all was still as death."*

Frozen in terror, the men dropped their brooms and fled through the snow to the powerhouse, their faces white and their breaths gasping. Their comrades laughed—at first. But when the motorman, the one who'd seen the ghost before, stepped forward and quietly confirmed their story, the laughter stopped.

Even the skeptical ones now passed the Curve with "bated breath and swelling heart," unsure what they might see… or hear.

And Now

The Black River Bridge and the old Cottesbrooke Curve have long been buried beneath pavement and intersection lights. Most who drive it today know nothing of Edwin Garvin, whose body was crushed beneath the iron carcass of a train.

But some still see someone standing at the edge of the intersection. Just a figure. Just a shadow. Waiting where no one should be. They blink. It's gone. They tell themselves it was nothing. Fatigue. Imagination.

But it isn't. And if you ever hear the faint rattle of rails on a road where no tracks remain…

Or the cry of someone still dying after all these years…

Don't stop. Don't look. And for God's sake—don't listen too long. Because some collisions never stop echoing. And the dead don't always stay buried beneath the rails.

The Gore Orphanage Horror
(Lorain County)

In Amherst, they say Old Man Gore nailed the doors shut and set the orphanage on fire—children screaming, pounding with tiny fists as flames swallowed their beds. That part isn't true. But what really happened may have been worse. In the early 1900s, John Sprunger—a wealthy industrialist cloaked in evangelism—bought up farmland near Gore Road and opened the Light and Hope Orphanage. Behind its saintly name was a machine of greed and cruelty.

He and his wife Katie used children like livestock—over a hundred boys and girls, some as young as seven—forced into slave labor under the guise of "learning trades." They weren't taught. They were beaten.

They didn't play. They starved. Some were rented out to local farms. Others slept among lice, rats, and rotting food. Their medicine? Prayer.

Their punishment? Whippings.

By 1909, children were escaping—running into Amherst and whispering their nightmares. Locals helped them flee in secret, creating an underground railroad for abused orphans.

Then came the fire.

In 1910, a massive explosion ripped through the orphanage's three-story print shop. Flames lit the sky. Official records say no children died. But no real count was ever kept. And the silence afterward—no investigations, no autopsies—still reeks of cover-up.

The orphanage shut down in 1916. The mansion burned again in 1923. And what remains now are bones beneath the soil, rumors in the trees, and voices that do not belong to the living.

People still visit the ruins. Some swear they've heard a child's voice whisper "Tryphenia," the name of a Swift girl buried nearby. Others say they've seen the ghost of a little girl swinging from a tree or found tiny handprints smeared across baby-powdered car windows.

So, go. See for yourself. But don't be surprised if something follows you back— still waiting for someone to let them out.

Pop Meyers Still Walks the Cherry Street Bridge
(Lucas County)

It's known today as the Martin Luther King Bridge, spanning the Maumee River and linking Cherry Street to Main in Toledo. But in its earliest form, long before concrete and steel, it was a simple wooden toll bridge called Cherry Street Bridge, built in 1865.

It cost two cents to walk across. Ten cents for a horse.

And the price some paid was far greater.

A Death Without Struggle – August 1882

In the suffocating heat of an August morning in 1882, a group of men walking home from duty stopped cold at the first pier of the old wooden bridge.

"I was horrified to see the body of someone hanging there," said Detective Louis Trotter. "It did not take us long to cut the corpse down, and we found it was Pop Meyers, as he was familiarly called."

Joseph "Pop" Meyers, a local shoemaker, had taken his own life—hanged by rope from the bridge. He had dressed carefully: a new shirt, fresh collar, and a clean necktie. But he wore no coat. No shoes. Just bare feet dangling above the river below.

"His face was just as pleasant as if he were selling a pair of shoes to a customer," Trotter recounted. "There was not the least sign of pain, and his wide-open eyes were looking rather expectantly up the river."

The Rope Returned

Soon after, Meyers' grief-stricken son came to the police. He begged them for the rope. "'I want it as a reminder,' he said, 'of my father.'" He got what he asked for. And not long after—at the very same spot, using the same rope—he followed his father into death.

The Man in Bare Feet

It wasn't long before people crossing the bridge began reporting something strange. A figure—silent, slow-moving—appearing in the dead hours after midnight.

"A nicely dressed man dragging a rope… no sound was made. His feet were bare, just as the police officers had found him."

The apparition mirrored the exact details of Meyers' death, down to the clothing, the bare feet, and the length of rope trailing behind him. "I investigated the affair and found it was true—something was haunting the bridge," Detective Trotter confirmed. "The ghost was dressed just as Meyers was the morning I cut him down."

New Bridge, Same Ghost

In 1884, the wooden bridge was torn away by flood.

A new steel bridge was constructed to replace it. But the ghost remained. "The first night the new bridge was opened," Trotter recalled, "wayfarers were badly frightened by a phantom walking slowly in his bare feet, making no noise as he softly trod the planks."

The years passed. Another bridge came in 1914. And yet another in the modern day. But no matter how many layers of stone, steel, or time were laid over the river—he still walks. Many people would divulge to police that they had seen Meyers' ghost patrolling the bridge, rope in hand, after midnight.

When the Fog Rolls In

On fog-drenched nights, when the Maumee hangs low with mist, drivers sometimes glimpse him—a man in dress clothes with no shoes, dragging something behind him. Sometimes, he turns to look. And sometimes... he keeps walking, silent and slow, fading back into the river haze. The Cherry Street Bridge may have changed its name. But the dead don't care for names. And as long as people must cross the Maumee, he'll be waiting.

Barefoot. Rope in hand. Looking up the river as if searching for the next one to join him.

The Lively Ghost
(Madison County)

Nora

Around 1862, a farmer and self-professed spiritualist took up residence near the old churchyard with his family near London, Ohio. Among the household was a young servant girl named Nora. She was beautiful, with bright eyes and dark hair often caught loose in the wind. The farmer's son had eyes for her.

Whether he used her, loved her, or simply toyed with her heart, no one can say.

Whatever passed between them ended in ruin.

One gray morning, they found Nora's body swaying from a plum tree, her nightdress soaked with morning dew, her bare feet dangling just above the orchard grass. Her neck stretched unnaturally to one side, the wind catching the tips of her hair like it meant to carry her away.

There was no ceremony. No marker. Just a rough wooden box dropped into a hollow among the weeds where the forgotten dead lay. As the days passed, the grave sank. The coffin collapsed inward. Soil shifted. Worms found their way in. Her flesh darkened and split.

The house went silent after that. But the land did not.

The Ghost in the Thickets

They say you can still see her.

A pale figure in the tall grass. A girl, barefoot, hair like smoke, face twisted with sorrow. She walks near the overgrown cemetery, sometimes by the roadside. Sometimes, you'll see her out of the corner of your eye, just past the thicket line—until you blink and she's gone.

Sometimes, she's hanging again.

And sometimes… her feet touch the ground.

The Stones That Came Inside

Not far from the orchard, Mr. Harlan P. Wood kept a neat farmhouse. He believed, at first, that some discharged worker was harassing him—throwing stones at his windows by night. But when no man was found, and the stones began to fly inside the house, his certainty broke.

As reported by the Fort Worth Daily Gazette, March 29, 1887: "Stones and bricks continued to fly through the sitting room window... some even hurled outward by unseen hands."

That was only the beginning. Clover seeds began to rain from nowhere, scattering across rooms like whispered curses. Potatoes, stored safely in the cellar bin, were later found heaped neatly in the sitting room upstairs, arranged with eerie care. Then, the constable came.

The Binding in the Cellar

Constable Donohoe entered the cellar that evening with a lamp and a pistol. He believed someone was hiding there. He was wrong. They say the lamp fell first. Then came the sound—a struggle, muffled grunts, and dragging feet. When they found him, Donohoe was tied hand and foot—his mouth stuffed with clover seeds, his eyes packed with them, too, as if to blind him from seeing whatever had come for him. And whatever it was... had done it silently.

The Land Still Waits

Today, the farmhouse is long gone. The orchard is skeletal. The graveyard remains choked with weeds. No sign marks Nora's resting place. No stone carries her name. But when fog crawls low across the fields, and the wind shifts cold through the thickets, some say you can still hear the sound of something swaying from the old tree— or the soft scrape of seed scattered on the cellar floor. Don't linger. Because the land has not forgotten.

And neither has Nora.

The Broken Thing on the Tracks
(Mahoning County)

There's a stretch of old track that runs from Hazelton Yard toward Struthers—just a single, rusting line now mostly used to haul garbage. But in the age of steel and soot, when furnaces glowed orange and trains screamed through the Mahoning Valley night, that rail line fed the industrial veins of Youngstown.

Men worked it by day.

But no one wanted to walk it at night. They whispered of something that crawled those rails. Something that once died there—and never quite stayed dead.

The Rail That Breaks Men

Back in the late 1800s, crews assigned to this stretch rarely lasted long. Some quit. Others went mad. A few were found bloodied or dead beside the rail bed, their injuries so unnatural they seemed less struck by steel than torn by fists of stone.

The blame always fell on one thing:

The Ghost of the Mangled Man.

They said he was once a worker—hulking, proud, a man built for rail and steel. But something happened. A misstep. A mistimed crossing. The scream of an engine, the thunder of impact, and then silence. What they pulled from the tracks was hardly a body—just twisted limbs, a crushed ribcage, and a skull that lolled like it had come loose from its spine.

Some say he was buried. Others say they never found enough to bury. But he came back.

Van Horn's Walk

One such tale survives. A rail worker named Van Horn—new to the job, unaware or unafraid of the stories—was tasked with walking the rails between Hazelton and Struthers on a moonless night. His only company: the cold air, creaking trees, and the thin yellow flicker of his lantern.

Then he heard it. Something moving. Low and wet, like dragging meat across gravel.

Van Horn turned, expecting an animal—maybe a drunk or a stray dog. Instead, he saw a shape crawling along the track. Not walking—crawling, rolling, its bones crunching and snapping as it moved. The closer it came, the more human it became.

But *wrong*.

Its limbs were too long, bent in the wrong places, folding and unfolding with sickening pops. Its head flopped side to side like it had no neck at all—just loose sinew. And its hands—those fists—were mottled, blackened, rotting.

Then it rose.

Half-standing. Mangled. Grotesque.

Van Horn tried to run, but the thing was on him—swinging its swollen, rotted fists with inhuman force. Each blow landed like iron. The light from his lantern flailed as he fell beneath it, screaming. By the time he stumbled into Struthers, bruised and nearly broken, he collapsed in the street, rambling of a "dead man walking wrong."

He never walked the line again.

The Thing That Returns

Over the years, others have reported seeing something crawling along that lonely stretch of track. A man-shaped form, hulking and twisted, dragging itself out of the gravel—only to vanish when approached.

A few say it runs beside slow-moving trains, keeping pace for a time. Others swear it tries to board, its bobbing head visible in the corner of a boxcar before fading into mist.

And some still say—quietly—that the deaths on that track weren't accidents. Not all of them.

That one of the dead came back, angry, and walks the rails to break the living the way he was broken.

So if you find yourself near Hazelton Yard after dark...and if you hear something behind you on the gravel...don't look back. Because it doesn't walk like a man. And if it catches up—it won't stop hitting until your bones sound like his.

One-legged Ghost of a Shoestring Peddler
(Marion County)

In the summer heat of 1909, whispers clawed their way through the iron bars of the Marion Jail.

Prisoners, sleep-deprived and wide-eyed, spoke in low voices of the thing that haunted the cells at night—the ghost of a one-legged shoestring peddler, known bitterly among them as Shoestring Jack.

Shoestring Jack's Demise

Six months earlier, Jack had been thrown into Cell 1, a filthy holding pen with peeling walls and no light. He'd been arrested for loitering, vagrancy, and bothering the good people of Marion with his wild eyes and handfuls of laces. No one thought much of him until they found him—swinging.

He had tied two of his shoestrings together, looped them over a bent pipe above the cot, and choked himself into silence. It was said his tongue turned black, and his glassy eyes stared upward—hopeful, almost—as if watching something crawl down from the ceiling to take him.

They buried him in Potter's Field.

But he never really left.

The Ghost's Unrest

Above the jail, in the cramped quarters of the city firefighters, Ira Shrock tried to sleep. But most nights, he was awakened by a slow, scraping rhythm beneath the floorboards:

Crunch. Drag. Crunch. Drag.

The sound of a wooden leg grinding over gritty cement. A pause. Then footsteps—soft, wrong, as if one heel were bare and rotted, the other hard and hollow like dry bone.

Then came the whispering.

Sometimes, Ira heard it muttering near the vent grates. Sometimes, it came from inside the walls.

Sometimes, from inside his dreams.

More than one man saw Shoestring Jack. Pale, slack-jawed, eyes sunken too far into his skull. He walked the corridor between the cells and stood longest outside Cell 1, dragging something behind him—a twisted noose of shoestrings, still frayed from the weight of his death.

He Still Walks

The jail is gone now. So is the firehouse. Both were torn down to make way for a parking lot at South Prospect and West Church Streets. But the haunt remains.

Some say on cold nights, long after the shops shut and the streets go silent, a sound still creeps across the concrete:

Crunch. Drag. Crunch. Drag.

And if you glance in your rearview mirror before driving away, you might catch a glimpse of something crooked stepping from the dark corner of the lot, twitching its head to the side, lifting a tangle of old laces—and smiling.

Bobbing Lantern Light
(Medina County)

For years, the locals have passed along that if you linger long enough in the Spencer cemetery, you'll see a lantern bobbing through the headstones—gliding at chest height, clutched in ghostly fingers that vanish in the dark.

Sometimes, a smaller light flickers beside it, keeping pace with it.

And if you're brave enough to step close, you can reach right through the glow.

Ghost Lights of the Cursed Sliding Hill
(Meigs County)

A River That Twists Like a Knife

Between the close-knit towns of Hartford City and New Haven, West Virginia—just across the Ohio River from Syracuse—there lies a bend so sharp, so treacherous, it has carved more than stone. It's carved fear.

They call it Sliding Hill.

Where the river kinks at a brutal right angle, the waters crash against stone with violent speed. In the age of steamboats, pilots cursed the place. Many didn't make the turn. And some never left at all.

Dancing Lights, Dead Eyes

Since the 1700s, witnesses from riverboats and roadside wagons alike reported phantom lights gliding along the hillside. Lanterns, bobbing without bearer. Skeletons glimpsed in bursts of lightning. Ghosts, they said, searching. Or guarding.

In 1910, a shanty boat family moored at dusk on the Ohio side, unaware of Sliding Hill's stories. As night thickened, the father noticed a light—drifting, dipping—on the West Virginia slope. Suspicious, he took a skiff and crossed.

What he saw turned his blood cold: A headless, hulking form heaving boulders with monstrous strength, its shoulders slick with rot and steam.

He fled. The family cast off and never looked back.

The Vanishing Horseman

Before the lights, before the monster, there was the rider.

In 1856, ten-year-old George Cleaton Wilding, a future Methodist circuit preacher, walked the narrow bridle path between Hartford and New Haven. At a stream crossing, a colonial officer on horseback approached him—majestic, silent, resplendent in uniform and shining blade. George looked down to hop the creek.

When he looked up, the rider was gone. No hoofbeats. No trace. Nothing.

Blood for Gold

The legend's heart is buried in greed.

Early settlers once camped at Sliding Hill, hauling with their sacks of gold coins—meant for land purchase. But word spread. Thieves followed. In the dead of night, they slit throats and stuffed the bodies in a stone ledge, burying the coins deep within the hill. They pushed the boat downstream to cover the crime.

But curses do not sleep.

One by one, the murderers died—mysteriously, violently. On his deathbed, one confessed.

The gold was never found.

The Curse of Sliding Hill

Since then, the hill has never rested.

Those who search for the gold don't return whole—if they return at all.

Some say their bones feed the brambles, tangled in roots that whisper at night.

Others still walk—hollow-eyed and crumbling, caught between death and the last greedy breath they took. They flicker in and out of the fog, lanterns swaying, their mouths frozen open in the shape of a question:

Where is it?

So if you see the light on Sliding Hill—don't follow.

Don't call out. And whatever you do…don't dig.

Unless you want to feed the hill.

Unless you want to be one of them.

The Vanishing at Tomlinson Cemetery

(Mercer County)

They say if one person stands in the center of Tomlinson Cemetery while another walks backward around the graves… the one in the center disappears. No one knows where they go. Across the road, the crumbling church remains. Locals still hear footsteps pacing the rotted floorboards inside—said to belong to the Sunday School superintendent who dropped dead mid-lesson.

The Ghosting Chair at Fletcher Cemetery
(Miami County)

In the 1800s, families sat in mourning chairs beside graves—quiet places for grief. The Duncan family's chair still waits at Fletcher Cemetery. But some say it's cursed.

They call it the Ghosting Chair. Sit in it, and you might not sit alone. A cold breath behind your ear. A hand on your shoulder. A voice asking why you disturbed them. Respect the chair. Or it might not let you leave. Ever.

Don't Look into Monroe Lake
(Monroe County)

At Monroe Lake near Jerusalem, look into the water.

They'll look back—drowned in the floods of Baker Fork, their faces press just beneath the surface—watching. Waiting.

Trapped in the still, dammed lake.

Don't stare too long.

Or you might join them.

Frankenstein's Castle Ghost
(Montgomery County)

Patterson's Tower rose from salvaged stone in the early 1940s—stitched together by boys from the National Youth Administration. They built it with condemned brick, torn from the guts of buildings that had already been sentenced to die. It stands tall, an observation post meant for blue skies and distant views. But they say stone holds energy from its past.

Especially stone that came from places never meant to rest easy.

The Decay and the Dare

By the 1960s, the tower was a husk. A haunted ruin tucked into the overgrown brush. The roof—peeled like old skin. The windows—gouged out. Graffiti sprawled like curses across the interior walls. Guards installed iron gates and heavy locks to keep out vandals and the curious. But those who wanted in always found a way.

They kicked bricks loose. Crawled through holes.

And dared each other to climb.

The Lightning Girl

On one such night in 1967, the sky cracked open with fury. Seventeen-year-old Ronnie Stevens and sixteen-year-old Peggy Harmeson slipped past the gate and into the tower, giggling and soaked, fleeing the rising wind. They climbed the long stairwell as thunder pulsed through the walls.

Peggy stood on the outer landing, peering into the storm, when the lightning found her. The strike lit the whole sky—and then silence. Ronnie woke in a splintered corner with the taste of iron in his mouth and blood trickling from his ears.

Peggy was sprawled on the landing, her limbs at wrong angles, her eyes burned wide open. They say her skin split at the touch of the lightning. They say her mouth was still forming his name.

What Still Climbs the Steps

Since that night, something walks the tower during storms. Locals say it appears when the rain turns to needles, and the thunder won't stop rolling—just a figure staggering down the winding stairs.

Its arms twitch. Its hair hangs wet and long over its face. Its footsteps slap and drag on the stone until it vanishes mid-step.

Some say it's Peggy, still trying to reach the bottom.

Others claim it's not her anymore—just what's left.

A husk burned hollow.

Moving because it doesn't know how to stop.

So, If You Visit Patterson's Tower

And the air smells like copper...and the lightning flashes without thunder—don't climb. Don't call out.

And if you see someone standing on the steps ahead—don't follow. She died seeking shelter from the storm.

But the tower betrayed her.

Now it waits for someone else.

Bessie Little Walks the Bridge
(Montgomery County)

Stillwater's Current Holds Its Secrets

A modern bridge on Ridge Avenue in Dayton stretches over the calm waters of the Stillwater River. Bicyclists pass, and joggers breathe deep along the recreation trail, unaware of the chill that waits in the air. But others— those who know—keep their eyes on the center of the bridge. That's where she appears. A pale young woman. Wandering. Pacing. Vanishing. Some rush forward, thinking she's leapt into the river below.

But the water is always still. No splash. No ripple.

No body. Only silence—and the feeling that something awful has just happened. Or is about to.

The Body in the River

September 2, 1896 – Dayton, Ohio Beneath the Athletic Park Bridge

The sun hung heavy over Dayton in a blistering late-summer heatwave. E.L. Harper, a visitor from Cincinnati, had come to the river to cool off. As he eased into the water, something unnatural floated past. A shoe.

It bobbed and snagged on a twig—or so he thought. When he drew closer, Harper realized the truth.

It wasn't a stick. It was a swollen, rotted leg.

A woman's body. Her skin darkened and distended. The face beyond recognition. He screamed. He fled. He ran dripping to the boathouse, calling for help.

They dragged her bloated corpse to shore.

The Unseen Wounds—The First Mistake

Coroner Lee Corbin arrived with little ceremony. No signs of trauma, he said. Probably suicide. Drowning. No need for alarm. She was dead. That was all.

But then the blood came. Not from the body—she had no more to give. It came from the bridge.

The Combs in Blood. And the Name is Found

Three boys, roughhousing near the bridge, found them: Two tortoiseshell hair combs, tangled in blood. Pretty things. Feminine. Still glinting in the sun. That's when Eliza Little stepped forward. They were her daughter's. Bessie Little.

Cast Out and Pregnant

Twenty-three and disgraced. Bessie had been forced out of her mother's home for her affair with a man named Albert Frantz. He was only twenty but already cruel.

Bessie had told her landlady she was meeting Albert at Boulevard Park on August 27. She never came back.

Then, the Frantz family barn burned to the ground. His horse, his buggy—gone. And so was Bessie.

Death Revisited. She Did Not Drown

Surgeon Fred Weaver performed the second autopsy.

What Corbin missed, he found. Two gunshots to the skull. Execution-style.

Bessie was pregnant.

Albert Frantz had tried to wash his guilt down the Stillwater. But the river would not keep his secret. Albert Frantz was arrested, found guilty at a trial, and electrocuted for his crime.

And Then She Returned

Years later, the Ridge Avenue Bridge over the Stillwater was rebuilt—but to those who remember, it's still called the Bessie Little Bridge. Life moved on in Dayton. For most. But not for the young woman who was murdered and thrown from its edge into the dark water below. They buried Bessie Little at Woodland Cemetery.

But she never left. People still see her. Alone. Walking the bridge. She does not speak. She does not turn. She just walks. And sometimes, just behind, a man's shadow follows. Some believe it is Albert Frantz.

The Curse of the Marshal's Gun
(Morgan County)

McConnelsville, Ohio – 1905

It began in blood.

In September of 1905, under the gray shadow of twilight, a man named Wood Stuard waited in the alley behind Main Street, cradling madness in his hands. He believed the city marshal, Horace Porter, was stalking him—some phantom lawman sent to bring him down.

So he struck first. Stuard ambushed Marshal Porter and shot him dead in the dirt.

The town reeled. But when the judge examined Stuard, they found no motive—only madness. He was declared insane and carted off to an asylum, his mind too broken to hang. But the gun—remained.

A Dead Man's Keepsake

Years later, the murder weapon passed into the hands of Francis Parsons, a young attorney who locked it away in his office safe, perhaps as a curio. Perhaps as a warning. But death followed that weapon like a loyal dog.

Parsons would come to prosecute Mrs. Francis Allen for the murder of her infant child. During the investigation, a man named John Smith—who stumbled upon the baby's shallow grave on his own property—dropped dead from a heart attack just days later.

Dr. Lucius Culver, a respected physician and the state's key witness, collapsed in the courtroom. He had gone rigid, his mouth twisted, his tongue useless.

He died soon after, unable to testify, his corpse frozen in silent accusation.

Suicide in the Courthouse

Then came the final act. Parsons—by now gaunt, sleepless, tormented—opened the safe, removed the revolver, and placed its cold mouth to his own.

He pulled the trigger. The marshal's gun fired once more. Now, they say Francis Parsons still walks the courthouse halls, doomed to pace where justice and madness bled together.

His shoes click against the tile, stopping just behind you before vanishing down the corridor.

A Relic of Death

142 East Main Street

The cursed gun remains.

You can see it still—its barrel dark, its chamber emptied of bullets but heavy with death—at the Morgan County Historical Society on East Main Street in McConnelsville.

But don't stare for too long. Some say it whispers.

And some say it's still waiting to be fired again.

Dead Rider of Vails Crossroads
(Morrow County)

A Crossroads Known for Its Tavern

By 1839, Vail's Cross Roads in Morrow County was known for its tavern and its steady flow of travelers. The hotel operated by Benjamin and Mary Vail gave food, rest, and a bed to men on the move—traders, stock buyers, and settlers drifting through the Ohio hills. It was a place to pass through, a brief stop on a longer road.

But not everyone who arrived at the crossroads left it behind.

The Rider on OH-656

On dark nights along OH-656, where West Liberty–Mt. Vernon Road crosses the highway, a ghost rides horseback. He appears suddenly, never speaking, and travels a fixed route—about two miles before halting at the hard bend near Rich Hill–Bloomfield Road. There, just before the entrance to Bloomfield Cemetery, he disappears. Some see the outline of a man with a low-brimmed hat. Others swear there's nothing above the shoulders at all. But always, the horse lowers its head before vanishing.

The House Where No One Stayed for Long

In the 1850s, a man named Salo Bintern lived near the crossroads. His house was crooked and always seemed in the process of falling in. He lived there with his wife and four sons. Though he kept to himself, people noticed that his farm—lean and unproductive—somehow still gave him enough to buy what he needed. He came and went often without explanation. The neighbors gossiped but had nothing solid to say. Then, one day, a wealthy stock buyer arrived in town.

An Invitation to Disappear

The man stayed at the Vail Hotel and made inquiries about land. He had money and was looking to settle. Bintern introduced himself and offered to help find a good parcel. He invited the traveler to stay at his home that night so they could leave early and not disturb the other guests. The man accepted. He left the hotel with Bintern and never returned. The next morning, his horse was found loose along the road. The rider was gone.

The saddlebags were missing. Not long after, Bintern bought a new farm.

The Dying Man with a Secret

Many years passed. The house sank deeper into rot. And then a man came to the Morrow County Infirmary— a stranger, sick and near death. He asked for a place to stay until the end and gave no name. But when the staff told him he'd need to prove he was a local, he finally whispered it. Bintern. After two weeks in bed, he asked for a private meeting with the superintendent. What he confessed was held back until his death, just as he'd requested.

A Killer's Last Words

Salo Bintern admitted to the murder. He had bludgeoned the traveler in his sleep and hidden the man's belongings beneath the floorboards of the old house. After he died, the superintendent went to the ruin and found them—scraps of leather saddlebag buried deep in the dust, just where Bintern said they'd be. The evidence was indisputable. The story was true. But something remained unfinished.

A Ghost That Never Reached the Grave

Even with the confession, the ghost continued to ride. He follows the same two-mile stretch of road from the old crossroads to the cemetery bend. He rides toward a place where he never got to rest. Some say he's still trying to finish the ride he began so long ago. Others say he knows exactly where he's going, and that's the part that should worry us. Because not every grave is enough to hold the dead.

The Unearthed: The Ghost of Miss Arnold at Moxahala Cemetery
(Muskingum County)

The Pretty Corpse

She was a light in the town in Zanesville—a pretty, modest girl known only as Miss Arnold. By winter's grip in 1823, she had withered from a lingering illness, wasting away under heavy quilts while her family kept a bedside vigil, hoping for a miracle that never came.

They buried her at Moxahala Cemetery beneath a low stone and a cross carved soft as breath. Snow fell that day, covering the mound with a quiet that felt like sleep.

But Miss Arnold would not rest.

The Pale Feet in the Hay

Weeks later, Jake—the stableman who worked the property of a local Doctor Conant—stepped into the barn, pitchfork in hand. The horses were restless, hooves scraping at the straw. As he drove the fork into the bedding, he hit something soft. Then he saw it. Two pale feet. Tiny. Cold. Sticking out from beneath the hay like they had been grown there.

Jake's scream brought a rush of footsteps. One of the four medical students under Doctor Conant stormed in, face bloodless, jaw clenched. He told Jake to shut his mouth or lose his teeth. They sent him away. But Jake didn't sleep well that night—and while he tossed in his cot, the students came and dragged the body away.

The Ghouls in the Night

Jake could not keep the horror buried. He went to the authorities. And word spread like rot in a wound. A mob formed with torches, pitchforks, and shovels. They descended on Moxahala and clawed open Miss Arnold's grave. The coffin was there, torn open.

Empty. It was true. The young woman's corpse—pure, innocent, not yet cold in the eyes of the Lord—had been defiled.

Her body was stolen by those who sought to carve it up, limb by limb, in the name of science. However, there was no law yet in place for body-snatching.

They called them ghouls. And even ghouls walked free. To pacify the furious mob, the students were arrested not for robbing her grave—but for stealing the clothes she was buried in. The charges did not stick.

And Miss Arnold never came home.

She Still Searches

They say the girl walks the perimeter of Moxahala Cemetery on cold nights, her bare feet trailing frost. Her face is pale. Her fingers long and desperate.

She drifts from stone to stone, clawing at the soil like a dog, moaning softly beneath the trees.

Looking for her missing self.

Doctor Conant's Restless Grave

Justice came, but it was slow and sour.

After the old doctor died, the townsfolk never forgave him. His stone vault was pried open again and again—by vandals, by children, by those who believed evil should not lie in peace.

People stared in at his withered corpse, laughing.

The children played with his skull and kicked it through the grass like a toy. Again and again, it had to be buried. The June 11, 1944, Sunday Times-Signal in Zanesville reported: Doctor Conant's bones still stir.

Even in death, the ghoul was not granted rest.

Miss Arnold was never put back together. Her ghost walks still. Because you cannot bury a body that's been torn apart. And you cannot silence a soul that was stolen.

Do not visit Moxahala after dark. She may think you've come to return her pieces.

The Shadow That Fell From the Sky
(Noble County)

It was September 3rd, 1925.

The dirigible USS Shenandoah, sleek and silver, drifted across the Ohio sky like a visiting god—on a Navy publicity tour meant to dazzle the public below.

But the heavens turned against her.

A violent storm over Noble County tore her apart midair.

Screams echoed in the wind as the massive airship fractured into sections, her steel bones shrieking. The stern came down hard near Ava. Fourteen men died— some ripped from the sky, others crushed in twisted wreckage that smoldered in the autumn fields.

Locals still speak of what was left behind.

Not the debris.

The Shadow.

Travelers along I-77 near Ava say they've seen it—just before dusk. A looming shape gliding silently through cloudless skies, casting no reflection, making no sound. It hovers. It drifts. Then vanishes.

Some say it's the Shenandoah still flying her doomed course. Others say it's the souls, bound to the wind, reenacting the moment they fell.

If you drive that stretch after dark and feel your skin prickle—look up.

You might see the ghost of the USS Shenandoah.

Forever falling.

The Bugler of Johnson's Island
(Ottawa County)

The Dead Stayed Hungry

Johnson's Island lies quiet now, just a slip of land in Sandusky Bay, but its soil is steeped in misery. In 1861, the U.S. Army seized forty acres from Leonard Johnson to build a prison for the Confederate officer class.

It was meant to be temporary.

It never really ended.

From 1862 to 1865, thousands of Southern soldiers wasted behind its fences.

Disease festered in the water and crept through the barracks like a rat. Winter came howling off Lake Erie, and the wind tore flesh from frostbitten hands. Nearly two hundred of them died—most nameless now—and were buried on the north end in cold, shallow ground.

They were hungry. They died hungry.

Quarried Bones

Decades passed, and in the late 1800s, the island turned festive—briefly—a summer resort, then something worse. By the early 1900s, limestone quarrying took over, gouging into the island's bones. A small, crude village rose to house the workers—many of them Italian immigrants. It had a school, a tavern, and a post office, but it was never lively.

It was not a place for joy.

The men lived under the sound of picks and shovels and, beneath that—a constant low hum. Some swore it was just the wind. Others said it was something else. A tune.

The same tune, over and over.

Dixie from the Grave

In 1915, during a storm that tore limbs from the shoreline trees, several laborers stumbled home from the quarry, soaked to the bone and weary. As they passed the old Confederate cemetery, one of them froze.

He pointed. Others turned.

The statue—the granite soldier with the bugle—was no longer facing the bay.

He had turned.

Facing his own dead, he lifted the bugle to his lips and let out a high, reedy note that cracked the night wide open. Mist curled from the lake like breath from an open grave. Then they came—ghostly soldiers— gaunt and wet, their eyes blank and their uniforms rotted, marching in step toward the woods beyond the camp.

They didn't look at the men.

They didn't need to.

Their song was for the living now.

Don't Listen Too Long

The old-timers said if you listened too long, the tune would follow you. That even in broad daylight, you'd hear "Dixie" drifting low across the water like it was coming from beneath it.

And if you heard the bugle again—God help you.

Because the statue doesn't always turn back.

And the dead don't always march away.

South Bass Island Lighthouse: The Keeper in the Cellar
(Ottawa County)

A Lighthouse Built on Isolation

In the summer of 1897, the South Bass Island Lighthouse opened its eyes to Lake Erie. Red-bricked and proper, it was meant to be a guardian—its beam slicing through storms to keep ships from splintering on the reefs. But charm and purpose couldn't keep out what was coming.

Harry Riley was the first to tend the light. A steady hand. But it was his hired caretaker, Samuel Anderson, who would become part of the island's darker legacy.

Beneath the Surface

Samuel was a reclusive man, soft-spoken and strange. He chose to sleep in the damp, stone cellar beneath the lighthouse—just wide enough for a cot, a stove, and his growing collection of snakes.

Locals said he spoke to them. Named them. Let them curl around his boots as he read old newspapers by lamplight. The cellar creaked with each gust off the lake. From below, he could hear the groan of ice breaking in the night. The whisper of wind through brick. The slow, steady rhythm of something alive in the pipes.

Then came the disease.

The Quarantine

In the fall of 1898, smallpox crawled across the lake like a fog. Towns quarantined. Ferries stopped. Soldiers patrolled the docks of Put-In-Bay, ordered to trap the infected where they stood.

Samuel panicked.

He slipped from the island, trying to cross the frozen water in a borrowed rowboat. But they caught him before he reached the mainland.

Dragged him back by his coat, past the lighthouse, past the snow-bitten pines, and locked him once more in his hole in the ground.

He stopped eating.

He stopped sleeping.

The Cliff

One morning, they found him. His body lay crushed against the limestone cliffs, ribs broken, eyes frozen wide. No one knew how he escaped the cellar. No one knew why the snakes were gone.

Some said he jumped.

Others swore they saw something crawling up from the rocks that night, moving like it had too many joints.

What Remains

Today, the lighthouse still stands.

Visitors speak of the basement—a room sealed off but not silent. Some sounds shouldn't exist: the slither of scales across stone, a breath that comes from behind you, and the sudden pressure of cold fingers on your ankle as you descend the stairs.

At night, some have seen a pale shape along the cliffs, watching the tower with empty eyes.

And when the wind is just right, the lighthouse groans... like something is still trapped beneath it.

Ghostly Remains of the Eaton Family Children's Home
(Paulding County)

Built for the Forgotten

In 1925, on a stretch of windblown land off Coffin Road in Paulding County, the Eaton Family Children's Home was built. Levi Eaton, long since dead, had kindly left his estate to the county with the intent to house the "orphans and indigent youth" of northwest Ohio.

They came in wagons. In shoes too big.

Some had no names worth remembering. But the home remembered them. It rose like a brick coffin on the hill. A school inside. A chapel. Rows of narrow cots where children cried into their sleeves at night. The place was meant for comfort, but even the staff whispered: "It always felt like it wanted more."

The Night the Sky Caught Fire

The storm came in hard one summer night. Wind screamed across the fields, and lightning lit the trees in blue veins. The home's roof was struck just before midnight. Flames spread fast. The halls filled with smoke. Wooden beams cracked. Something upstairs gave way.

Children were buried in ash and cinders. Some burned alive in their beds. By morning, the sky was clean.

But the windows still bled black.

The Names That Were Never Written

They never released the real number of dead. Some say six. Some say thirteen. A cemetery plaque now stands where the home once stood. The names carved are few, mostly of the family.

Voices in the Ashes

If you walk the site near sundown, some say you'll hear a cough.

But others hear raspy-throated singing, soft and cracked, like a lullaby hummed through soot—

Bloody Horseshoe Grave
(Perry County)

A Sign From the Saddle

James Kennedy Henry was a farmer and early settler, born in 1814—a quiet man with callused hands and two women tangled around his heart. He couldn't choose between them: Mary Angle, delicate and clever, and Rachael Hodge, bold and full of laughter. One chilly night in 1844, riding home under the stars, James dozed off in the saddle. When he opened his eyes, the horse had stopped—hooves planted before Mary Angle's door.

He took it as a sign. Fate had chosen. James obeyed.

The Wedding Gift

James and Mary married in January, beneath pale skies and bare trees. As was tradition, both sets of parents gifted the couple something to start their new life: a pair of strong workhorses. A team to till the fields. A future harnessed in leather and muscle.

But fate has a cruel hand.

Mary bled out giving birth to their first child in February 1845. James buried her in a lonely corner of Otterbein Cemetery, the ground too hard to dig, the grave too shallow.

He returned home broken.

But he did not return the horse.

Whispers Beneath the Soil

Tradition demanded it. If a bride died before giving life to the marriage, her dowry was to be returned.

James kept the horse. Mary's family, ruined by illness and bad crops, needed the animal. But no one spoke of it aloud—only the wind carried the whispers. *The Henrys are greedy. That horse is cursed.*

Three years passed. James remarried.

He returned to Rachael, now 22, and they wed in spring. But when James visited Mary's grave to make peace with the past, something had changed.

The Mark

Etched—no, burned—into the back of Mary's headstone was a shape that hadn't been there before:

A blood-red horseshoe.

The stone bled from within. He scraped at it, tried to wipe it clean. But the iron shape remained. Some nights, it dripped. And though Rachael bore him four daughters and filled the house with warmth, James never looked at the barn the same way again.

Because one of those horses still lived.

And it watched him.

The Hoof That Waited

It came on a Friday night. The sun had just dropped below the trees. James was in the barn, feeding the horses. One turned. Quietly. No noise. No warning.

And kicked.

The blow crushed the side of his head.

The horse didn't bolt. It just stared.

It was the very horse gifted by Mary's parents—the one that should have been returned. The one they said was cursed.

They buried James.

The horseshoe is still there.

Blood darkened and dry now, it still appears fresh, as if stamped anew by something hooved and unseen.

Ghost Horses of Stage's Pond
(Pickaway County)

What the Storm Brings

When storms creep across the flatlands of Stages Pond State Nature Preserve, an old-growth forest with ancient glacial ponds, the air turns heavy—like something unseen is pressing down on the earth. That's when it begins. First, a distant rumble. Not thunder—hooves.

Galloping. Slamming. Churning the mud.

Then, the splash—violent and deep—like a heavy wagon careening off into the marsh.

And finally...screams.

Not human. Not animal.

Something between.

Visitors have stopped in their tracks, frozen mid-step, trying to place the sound. But it vanishes—swallowed by the bog as if it never was.

But it was.

The Storm That Took Them

It happened long ago—when a farmer on Ward Road was out raking hay. The day was stifling. Sweat stuck to his collar, and the clouds hung low. Then—lightning ripped across the sky.

Thunder cracked the ground. And the horses spooked.

His wagon team bolted, eyes wide with panic, foam flecking their jaws. They galloped out of control, down the hill, across the low road—and straight into the black maw of the marsh at Stage's Pond.

Locals came running to help the farmer. They found churned mud. A harness. A broken wheel. But no horses. No wagon. Only bubbling muck, slowly swallowing the last sliver of wood into the earth.

The Echo That Walks Ahead

Now, when lightning flashes and thunder shudders over the preserve, those near the water say they feel it: A tremor in the ground. The thump of hooves. Then, the screams. And always the splash. Heavy. Final. Drowning.

No footprints. No broken reeds. No ripples. Just silence thick as syrup—and a smell, faint but rotting.

The Haunted Stump
(Pike County)

Where Fire Devoured the Living

Before Pike Lake was a park, it was wilderness—dense and brambled. When a farmer needed to clear a patch for a cabin or a cornfield, word would spread. The neighbors came. Men. Women. Children. They all worked. Axes rang out through the trees. Trees fell. Limbs were chopped. Stumps were ripped. With handspikes and sweat, the community dragged logs into high stacks. At night, the whole place burned like hell had surfaced.

They called it a log rolling—a fire-fed festival of labor and fellowship.

And sometimes, fire demanded more than wood.

The Woman at the Fire

It was in the 1860s, during one of the larger clearings near where Pike Lake State Park is now located.

One young woman, just eighteen, worked a fire line with the rest. She had smoke in her eyes, calluses on her palms, and a long stick in her hand to shift and settle the burning pile. They'd built it tall—limbs and trunks blackened to coal at the base, tongues of flame licking higher with every breeze.

She moved around the edge, poking and prodding, sweat streaking the soot on her cheeks. Then it happened. A sound like bones snapping—a flaming log from the top broke loose.

She turned just in time to see it falling. Her stick jammed beneath its weight, and before she could release it—the log pulled her down.

She hit the earth.

Her palms slapped the dirt. The burning log rolled over her hands, her wrists, and her screams.

The Stump That Took Them

Help came fast, but the fire was faster.

They found her writhing, sobbing, black smoke curling from her sleeves. She clutched the air like her hands were still attached—but they weren't.

The heat had cooked the flesh to ash.

Her hands fell off.

Dropped like wet bark onto the tool stump nearby—two shriveled, blistered things still shaped like fists. She died in the weeds while the fires crackled around her.

The pile burned down.

The trees were cleared.

But the stump—the one that caught her hands—remained.

The Grasp From Below

Years passed. The clearing became woods again. Trails were cut. A state park came to be. But those who walk the deeper paths near the old rolling site say it still feels wrong.

Some speak of something skulking and scrambling from beneath the crackling leaves.

Two blackened hands.

Crawling blindly up the stump.

Wristless. Grasping.

Others say they feel a searing clutch around the ankle—just for a moment—hot and sharp, like coals wrapped in fingers.

The Crying Girl of Twin Lakes
(Portage County)

The Lakes That Were Never Still

Just northeast of Kent in Portage County lie the Twin Lakes—two quiet bodies of water once ringed by cabins, cottages, and winding paths. In the early 1900s, this was a place where families escaped the summer heat, where children ran barefoot down dirt roads, and where the water always seemed to carry a hush, even on windless days. However, for generations, locals have reported a weeping sound that echoes across the lake at dusk.

Not animal. Not wind. Something human. Something childlike.

A Thin Winter and a Girl on the Ice

One version of the story begins in the winter of an unrecorded year, sometime in the early 20th century. A young girl—her name long forgotten—was said to be playing near the shore when her dog ran out onto the ice. She followed, calling to it, laughing as the dog barked and spun. But the ice that year was thin. Too thin. And when she reached the middle, it broke.

No one saw it happen. They only found the dog, wet and shivering at the bank, and a wide hole where the black water opened like a wound. Her body was recovered two days later. Frozen. Eyes open. Mouth slightly parted as if she'd been screaming when the lake silenced her.

The Weeping on the Shore

It began not long after. People walking the wooded trails near the water reported hearing crying—soft, high-pitched, and distant. They would pause, listening, but it always stopped the moment they moved closer. In winter, some claimed to see small wet footprints along the frozen banks, leading toward the middle of the lake and vanishing at the edge of the ice. In rare cases, those who lingered said they saw something beneath the surface—pale and still—just below their feet.

The Girl Beneath the Ice

As the story spread, more details attached themselves to it. Some say she's still chasing her dog. Others believe she's searching for someone to save her.

A few say she doesn't know she's dead.

Those who've seen her describe a thin figure crouched near the edge of the lake in a soaked nightgown, hair matted over her face, arms wrapped around her knees. She turns only when noticed—and vanishes before she stands.

In one version, if you hear her cry and answer it, she appears in the water behind you. Not reflected. Present.

Where the Water Remembers

Though cabins have come and gone, though the old roads have been paved and the shoreline cleared for homes, the crying has never stopped. Those who live near the lakes still report strange sounds at night. Some leave offerings on the shore—ribbons, flowers, stuffed toys—for a girl with no name and no grave. She is part of the lake now, and the lake has never given her up.

So if you're near Twin Lakes on a winter evening and hear a child crying beyond the reeds—don't follow.

The ice breaks fast.

And nothing that sinks beneath its frozen depths ever comes back the same.

The Witch's Grave at West Branch State Park

(Portage County)

Portage County's Lost Cemetery

In the tangled woods of West Branch State Park, hidden beyond overgrown paths and washed-out logging roads, lies what remains of the Elliott Family Cemetery.

The stones are few, sunken and choked with vines, lost to the world and time.

The place was discovered in the 1920s by the Elliott Lake Club as they cleared ground for a recreation area—though they cleared little here. What they found was old and still, as if the woods had swallowed it on purpose. A cemetery without a church. A family burial ground once belonging to Mulford and Betsy Elliott, whose farmstead sat just across the creek. Now only a few bricks and bones remember their names.

They called it Portage's Lost Cemetery.

The name fit.

"What I Am, You Will Become"

In the center stood the grave of a girl—seventeen years old when she died. Her stone was thin and leaning, and time had eroded most of the words. But one part endured:

"Remember youth as you pass by,

As you are now, so once was I."

The line is ancient, borrowed from Latin epitaphs meant to unsettle, not comfort. A reminder not of peace, but of inevitable decay. Her grave always seemed colder than the others.

The weeds thicker. The soil unwilling to take seed. Some believed her death had not been natural. Others said she wasn't truly dead at all.

And across the creek… the stories began.

Stones to Hold Down the Dead

Just beyond the waterline is a strange pile—massive, flat slabs too heavy for easy placement.

Locals long whispered it was no coincidence.

In old settler tradition, anyone suspected of witchcraft was denied burial in sanctified ground. Instead, they were forced into the edge of the woods and buried beneath stone, pinned down so they couldn't rise. The method was simple. Lay them out. Cover their body with boards. Place stone upon stone.

It was supposed to be final.

But the dead don't always stay buried.

The Desecration of 1969

In May of 1969, a group of vandals came looking for the graveyard. They brought beer and bravado. They smashed the headstones. Knocked over the girl's marker. Laughed at the old verse carved in weathered granite. When they crossed the creek and found the pile of stones, they jeered. Some claimed they heard knocking from beneath them. One boy tried to shift a slab and said he saw something—something wet and red behind the cracks.

They left in the dark.

They never spoke of what followed.

But within weeks, every one of them suffered. One was hospitalized after falling from a moving car. Another lost his job and spiraled into drugs. One boy disappeared altogether—last seen walking alone through West Branch just before dusk, muttering about eyes in the trees.

The One Who Walks There Now

The forest is quiet until it isn't. Hikers have reported a woman drifting between the trunks, her back arched wrong, her hands dragging the ground.

Some say she has no eyes. Others say she has too many.

And the girl from the grave—her presence is felt, even if not seen. The air grows still near her marker, and sometimes—just sometimes—you hear the dirt shift beneath your feet.

Some say the accused witch never truly died. That her body remains below the stone pile, twisted and waiting, her soul stuck somewhere between vengeance and decay. Her ghost walks the woods in the shape of what the townsfolk feared she would become. A revenant.

And if you peer too long into the cracks between the stones, you might see her eyes looking back—glassy and red, blinking slow as if just waking from the grave.

But others know the truth—she was never a witch.

Just a dead girl, silent in the soil, until vandals shattered her grave and tore the veil that kept her still. That's when she woke. And she's not a morning person. She is angry. Vengeful. Looking to take it out on whomever crosses her path.

She moves through the world of the living with a rage no witch ever knew—taunting, mocking, cursing, and latching onto anyone who dares disturb the veil between the dead and the breathing.

Don't go looking.

Don't mess with her grave.

Unless you want to end up like the vandals who started it all—hollow-eyed, silent, and missing.

The Curse of Devil's Backbone
(Preble County)

The Hill of Bones

Before it was a Preble County park, before it was mapped or marked, the high spine above Paint Creek was sacred. The Myaamia called it Backbone Hill—a burial site where they placed their dead with stone tools, feathers, and prayer.

They laid their warriors and elders along the ridge, earth packed with care, bones wrapped in quiet.

The hill was never meant to be disturbed.

But in 1794, General Anthony Wayne's army crushed the Myaamia resistance at Fallen Timbers. With the Treaty of Greenville came forced surrender. Among the signers was a Myaamia chief known as Red Turtle. He gave up his lands under pressure—but not his warning.

Before he left, he spoke plainly to the white settlers:

The dead will not rest.

And those who disturb them will suffer.

A String of Misfortunes

The years that followed brought quiet... but not peace. People living near Devil's Backbone told of strange misfortunes: children lost in the woods, plows that broke against buried stone, and men thrown from horses on clear paths.

One by one, they began to whisper: *Red Turtle's curse.*

The tales remained on the edge of belief—until Franklin Bourne disappeared.

The Vanishing of Franklin Bourne

In 1912, Bourne was a prosperous farmer and engineer. He lived alone near the Backbone, tending his land with precision. Around Easter, he vanished without a word. A hired man named Elwood Davis claimed Bourne had left for the South and asked him to sell the farm.

The neighbors were uneasy, but Davis had money, a bill of sale, and no blood on his hands. Not yet.

Unearthed

The body was found a year later—June 10, 1913—in a shallow grave three feet deep in Bourne's garden.

Wrapped in a blanket. Rotting. Skull shattered by a blow to the back of the head.

Elwood Davis was arrested for first-degree murder and confessed to the killing. He'd used an axe. Stole Bourne's money. Buried the corpse among the cabbages.

He was sentenced to the Ohio Penitentiary and died there in 1936. Justice, maybe.

But some say the axe was only part of the story.

The Second Curse

Bourne had been seen digging before he vanished—clearing a row near the edge of the Backbone. It's said he struck something hard, unwrapped in clay: a bundle of bones and stone beads, the remains of someone buried long before Ohio was a state.

He reburied it and said nothing.

That night, neighbors saw someone standing at the edge of his field. A tall, dark figure. Not Davis.

After the murder, the earth where Bourne fell grew wrong. The grass curled. Nothing sprouted. Even now, hikers say animals avoid that patch of ground. And hikers speak of a gaunt man with a ruined head who walks the ridge line at dusk—dragging one foot through the dirt as if hunting for something buried.

Red Turtle was right. The dead will not rest.

And neither will the ones who disturb them.

Bell Cemetery Soldier's Light
(Preble County)

Tucked in the quiet backroads of Preble County, Bell Cemetery dates back to the mid-1800s. Once surrounded by open fields, it's now enclosed by forest and farmland, a small patch of weather-worn stones watching the sky. Several Civil War veterans lie buried here, alongside early settlers whose names have long vanished from local memory.

But the dead are said to linger.

And they're not quiet.

The Blue Light and the Watcher

For decades, visitors have reported a strange blue or white orb floating through the cemetery after dusk. It flickers behind trees. It hovers near gravestones. Sometimes, it zips straight toward the car of anyone who dares linger too long, vanishing before impact.

Locals call it "the soldier's light."

Some say it's the restless ghost of a Union soldier whose body was never claimed, buried without ceremony. Others claim it's an unnamed child interred on the edge of the cemetery—its grave, once marked by a wooden cross, is now gone.

Alongside the light, people have heard:

- Footsteps on gravel with no one nearby
- Disembodied coughing or whispers
- The sensation of someone standing behind them, watching

Desecration and Return

In the 1970s, a rash of vandalism brought an eerie escalation. After gravestones were broken, the light reportedly grew brighter and more active—appearing not just in the cemetery but in the surrounding woods and even approaching nearby homes. Some believe those buried at Bell Cemetery were disrupted, and their spirits now guard the land. Those who mocked or disrespected it often found themselves plagued by odd misfortunes: car crashes, sudden illnesses, and unexplained accidents. Bell Cemetery doesn't just remember. It responds.

And if you see the blue light, don't follow.

Don't speak. Just go. Walk away. Run . . .

The Ghost on County Road 19
(Putnam County)

She appears at night—silent, unmoving—standing dead center in the road. Her dress is pale and stained. Her face is hidden in shadow. And the moment your headlights strike her... she's gone. But sometimes, she lingers longer. Sometimes, she watches.

Where She Haunts

Just northwest of Kalida, County Road 19 slices through farmland and timber. By day, it's empty. By night, it's a corridor of silence. That's when she comes.

A woman in white. Alone in the middle of the road.

No footsteps. No sound. Just a shape in the dark—until your tires swerve or your heart skips. Then, nothing.

Her Legend

The story's old. Some say she was a bride-to-be, struck and killed near the old tracks.

Others whisper about a girl thrown from a carriage on prom night. One version tells of a drowning.

None of the endings are happy. But every version ends with her walking back to where it happened, waiting for help that never came.

Why She Lingers

Some believe she's trapped in a final act of mercy—trying to warn drivers of their fate. Others say her death was never acknowledged.

No funeral. No name. Just a soul smeared across the blacktop like blood. She doesn't walk to safety. She walks to finish something.

Witness Warnings

A white dress flashes in headlights—too late.

She doesn't run. She stares, then disappears. Some see her farther up the road, walking—just at the edge of the ditch. One man said she touched his windshield. It iced over instantly.

The Unresolved Mystery

No one knows who she is. No missing persons file fits. No grave bears her name. But the sightings? They haven't stopped. Locals don't question it anymore. They just warn: Don't drive 19 alone after midnight.

The Spirits of Spooks Hollow
(Richland County)

It hides in the woods off a forgotten road—nothing but trees, wind, and the smell of wet stone. Locals call it Spooks Hollow, a ravine just east of Mansfield, and few walk there after sundown. The land looks ordinary enough, but the shadows fall longer here. Deeper. Heavier. They say it began in the years after the War of 1812. A tavern once stood near the edge of the hollow. That's where Seneca John and Quilipetoxe, two Delaware men, were last seen alive.

The Murder No One Confessed

According to scattered whispers and half-kept records, the two men had come in for drink and rest. What happened inside the tavern is still unclear. Some say a fight broke out.

Others claim they were accused of theft.

But by nightfall, they'd fled—or were chased—into the woods.

They never came back.

In the days that followed, farmhands found their bodies deep in the ravine, covered in rock and brush. But there was no trial. No investigation. No names were named—just silence.

And that silence rotted.

The Hollow That Watches

It started as rustling—leaves moving when there was no wind. Then came the voices. Low. Close. Speaking a language no one could place, but always just behind you.

Then, people began seeing them.

Two figures. Sometimes one. Drifting near the tree line, indistinct but human-shaped. Never moving quickly. Never speaking. But watching. Their eyes catch the moonlight like animal glass. Some say one points.

The Legend Grows Sharp Teeth

Throughout the 19th century, more than a dozen travelers reported a presence on the trail—sometimes blocking their way, sometimes following behind. One hunter claimed his lantern was extinguished three times in one night, though there was no rain, no wind.

He left the woods with scratches across his back and never went again.

By the 1930s, old-timers told their grandchildren: If you find yourself in Spooks Hollow, don't speak. Don't whistle. Don't answer if your name is called. Because it might not be someone living who's speaking.

A Warning Still Heard

There's no marker. No plaque. No grave. But the hollow remains. The name has outlasted the murderers. And the ghosts?

They haven't gone anywhere.

They want to be seen.

They want to be heard.

And they want what was taken.

Some places forget. Spooks Hollow remembers.

And if you wander there after dark, you will be remembered, too.

Black Dogs of Zeiter's Cemetery
(Richland County)

Where the Ground Won't Stay Quiet

Zeiter's Cemetery doesn't hide in the woods. It lies plain and visible—tucked beside Sheets Drive and Hoff, with farmland stretching wide to the horizon. By day, it's peaceful, barely noticed by passing cars—no iron gate. No chapel. Just a patch of headstones that catch the wind.

But by night, something waits there.

They say the land remembers what was buried without ceremony. What was hidden. What should have been left alone.

Whispers from the 1800s

By the late 1800s, rumors began to spread of howls on still nights, low and guttural, like wolves trying not to be heard. Livestock went missing. Dogs wouldn't enter the graveyard—one boy who wandered in found claw marks on a headstone—and no tracks leading away.

It was just an old cemetery, they said. But those who lived nearby kept their distance—something watched from the treeline. Something moved between the stones after dusk.

The Murder That Took Root

The legend grew darker after the Flora Farm incident in the early 1900s—a traveling peddler—never named—disappeared after visiting the farm just a mile from Zeiter's. The Flora family claimed he left on foot. But neighbors talked. Loud voices were heard. A struggle. And then silence. He was never seen again.

Months later, children picking berries near the cemetery found shredded cloth and old buttons in a patch of disturbed earth. A dog began digging and refused to stop. But the authorities dismissed it.

No body, no crime.

When the Dogs Returned

After that, the black dogs appeared. Large—too large. Thick-bodied, coal-colored beasts with red-tinged eyes that never blink. They'd stand between the stones and watch. Just watch.

Sometimes, they'd vanish mid-step.

Sometimes, they'd appear in your rearview mirror.

One farmer swore a dog followed him home, circling his house until dawn. He found muddy prints on every windowsill.

What They Protect

Folklore says these hounds are grave guardians, spirits of vengeance tied to an unmarked body. Some say they're what's left of the murdered peddler. Others believe the cemetery was built over older, unconsecrated land, and the dogs are its ancient sentries.

Whatever the case, those who see them often report misfortune within the week:

- Sudden sickness
- Broken bones
- Dreams of suffocation beneath the dirt

The dogs don't bark. They don't growl. They stare. And they never appear alone.

Final Warning

Zeiter's Cemetery is public, yes. But if you go, don't linger after the sun dips low. It isn't just that the law does not allow it. It is that the cemetery is haunted. Don't bring a flashlight—it won't help. And if you see a black shape between the headstones, turn around.

Because if you see one, the others are already behind you. And not all graves are meant to stay closed.

Crying Baby of Horseback Knob in Black Run Hollow
(Ross County)

The Grave Beneath the Pines

High on Horseback Knob, where the land humps upward like the spine of something buried, there is a single child's grave. No fence. No path. Just a moss-slick stone swallowed by roots set deep in the shade of old-growth pine. It has no name—just a date long worn away. Some say it marks the death of a baby lost in the winter of 1853. Others claim that no death was recorded at all.

But all who've found it agree on one thing:

It was not meant to be found.

The Cry in the Hollow

The locals call it a curse or a call. Just after dusk, hunters in the Black Run hollow have heard it—a faint baby's cry, thin and wet, drifting from the tree line. It stops the moment someone speaks. Step too close, and you'll find nothing there—only wind and stone.

Some see a pale figure toddling near the pines. Others see a flash of white at the corner of the eye, then feel a cold weight press against their back—as if someone small and unseen is riding their shoulders down the trail.

Why It Haunts

They say the family buried the infant there in secret, far from town, then left the valley for good. Whether it died of sickness or something darker, the child was laid on the earth with no rites and no name. And now its ghost lingers—not crying for help but for memory.

Those who find the grave often lose their way home.

Some return to their car with pockets turned out. Others forget entire hours. One man reported finding teeny prints beside his own—and they were barefoot.

Elizabeth's Grave: Where the Dead Don't Stay Still

(Ross County)

There's a cemetery hidden at the end of a winding lane outside Chillicothe—Mount Union-Pleasant Valley—a broken place in the shadow of new homes, oak trees, and shotgun shells. Vandals stripped its beauty, and even the Presbyterian church that once anchored it is gone. In its place: shattered monuments, gravestones heaped like garbage at the back fence, and something worse—dead that do not sleep quietly.

A Family Forgotten

Generations of the McCoy clan—some of the area's first settlers—lie buried here, or what's left of them. The land once pulsed with life: worshipers, homesteaders, mourners. Now, it's trampled by hunters and bored teenagers. Fast food wrappers mingle with crushed lilies. And yet, amid the wreckage, one name keeps returning.

Elizabeth.

Her stone was once proud beneath an old oak near the church. But the tree cracked in a storm—or was split by vandals—and her grave was desecrated. Caretakers moved the stone. Others tossed it in the rubble. Yet it returned. Always, it returned to that same place beneath the ruined tree.

The Ghost That Rises

Locals knew to park on Union Lane, kill the engine, and wait. If you stepped onto the grass, you ruined your chances. You had to remain outside the boundary.

Only then might you see it:

A low white mist rising from the tree line—slow at first, drifting like breath from a wound and then shaping into the form of a woman.

Elizabeth.

She would pass the edge of the vanished church, float beside the graveyard path, and pause beneath that beautiful old tree—where her stone belonged.

There, she lingered as if waiting for someone to set it right. And then she faded.

Unless, of course, you had moved the stone yourself.

A Gravestone That Refuses to Stay Dead

Those who dared to touch her marker—to shift it, to hide it—found themselves cursed. All of them spoke of the same thing before they had some horrible thing happen to them: a cold hand pressing down on their chest each night, heavier and heavier, as if a stone was being dragged across their lungs.

Final Word

The road to Elizabeth's Grave is no longer remote. The woods have thinned. The church is gone. But still... her marker moves. And the mist still climbs from the hollow on nights when the air is heavy with rot and memory.

So if you find yourself in Pleasant Valley Wildlife Area, and you come across a headstone alone beneath a tree, don't touch it. Don't even look at it too long.

Because some stones are not just carved with names.

They're carved with warnings.

The Dead and the Dungeon at Sandusky County Courthouse
(Sandusky County)

The Jail That Forgot the Light

Beneath the sandstone courthouse in Fremont lies a cramped stone passage with crumbling walls and rusted bars—the original county dungeon, dug by hand in the mid-1800s. It once held prisoners chained to walls without windows—their punishment was not just isolation but silence, filth, and endless darkness.

There are no windows. No sunlight. Only breath. And stone. And echoes. The air is still thick with rot.

The Forgotten Prisoner

Local lore says one prisoner was never recorded leaving. In 1871, a man accused of slaying a neighbor in cold blood was held here, pending trial. No final verdict, no newspaper mention after that.

The man vanished. Some say he hung himself in the cell and was buried outside town. Others insist a crooked deputy delivered justice early with his fists and a hemp rope. But the cell was scrubbed, the record wiped. And still—he walks.

Signs in the Stone

Tour guides don't speak of him unless pressed.

They'll mention the cold spots, sure. The footsteps echo through the corridor after everyone has left.

They won't tell you about the photo from 2014— a visitor posed beside the barred cell, and a gaunt face stared from the shadows behind, its mouth agape in a silent scream. Others hear breathing—labored, ragged, behind their shoulder, just as they descend the final step.

He Knows You're There

If you walk the corridor after dark, lights dim without cause. Phones die. Some visitors feel their sleeves pinched by unseen fingers. Once, a tour guide dropped her lantern when she felt a hand on her neck—but no one was behind her. What remains of him is anger and unfinished punishment. And a mouth that never stops whispering.

The Peddler's Grave in the Hollow
(Scioto County)

In a briar-choked hollow near Portsmouth—where the trees lean in too close, and even the birds fall silent—there lies a place the maps once marked only as Twin Creek Right Fork. Hidden between Little Gum Hollow and Webb Hollow in Shawnee State Forest, it is a place the wind rarely touches. What lies there is older than most are willing to admit. A grave. And something beneath it is still watching.

Bones in the Overhang

It was in the 1930s when CCC laborers cut a trail through the ravine. Under a shallow stone overhang, half-swallowed by moss and rot, they uncovered a nightmare. Human bones. Splintered, scattered. Nestled beside them were combs, bent tin plates, and worn tools—implements no man would carry except a traveling peddler, one who sharpened blades, patched pots, and traded trinkets to those buried deep in the woods.

But this peddler never left the hollow.

Marked by Death

The bones were gathered and buried beside the rock cleft, and a jagged, handmade stone set to mark the spot. Carved with a trembling hand, it read:

"H. T. Aug. 13, 1824. A.D., Dead M."

Nothing more. No name. No prayer. It's just the flat stamp of a violent end.

The Last Route

Elders began to murmur. They remembered stories— half-lost in time—of a peddler in the 1820s who passed through Buena Vista, a river town along the Ohio. He'd left for Upper Turkey Creek, a rugged journey northeast through six miles of unforgiving wilderness. But he never arrived.

No body was found. No inquiry. Only a silence that lingered too long. Some whispered murder. Others claimed he was gutted like an animal and stuffed beneath the stones. But no one in Friendship, or anywhere near, ever said it too loud. They knew better.

What Remains in the Hollow

For years, no one dared enter the hollow after dusk. Hunters swore they heard gurgling cries and choking gasps in the trees. Others claimed to hear metallic scraping as if tin cups still rattled inside a pack long forgotten.

Worst were the screams.

They did not echo. They rose from the ground.

Floodwaters eventually tore through Twin Creek, washing away the stone and what was left of the peddler's second grave. And when the waters receded, a bag of bone-handled trinkets and broken tools turned up among the roots, scattered like teeth.

Final Warning

The grave is still there, and the hollow still breathes.

If you pass between Little Gum and Webb Hollow at night and hear a whistle—don't answer.

If you see something glint in the brush, don't touch it.

Because the peddler may still be waiting beneath the rock, throat torn open, eyes still searching for the face of whoever led him there. And he wants his stuff back.

The Screaming Mimi of Seneca County
(Seneca County)

Murder at Midnight

They say it happened under a full moon. Midnight, maybe just after. A man—her new husband—led Mimi to the bridge, that one on CR 15 and TR 148. Some said she still wore her wedding dress. Others said she'd already changed. Either way, the lantern he carried lit the water below in long, sickly streaks.

No one knows what words passed between them. What promises he made. But they know what happened next. He raised the axe. One clean swing. He took her head. He hurled her body over the side—her blood still warm, still spurting—as if she were no more than trash. The axe and the lantern followed. With the river below silent and swallowing, he stood alone on the bridge.

And then he screamed. "MIMI!" Once.

"MIMI!" Twice.

"MIMI!" Three times—like a curse.

Then he climbed into his car, the headlights slicing through the darkness, and disappeared up the hill toward River Road. He was never seen again. Some say the guilt drove him mad. Others believe the river claimed him as well. His body was never found.

Return to the Bridge

Now, when the moon is full and the clock strikes twelve, the legend says Mimi walks. She rises from the black water beneath the bridge—her severed head held in one hand, the empty stump of her neck dark and gaping.

If you dare to stop your car off the road near the bridge, flash your lights, blow your horn, and scream "MIMI!" three times just like her killer did—she'll come for you.

Looking for him. Looking for revenge.

And if your face even remotely reminds her of his...she doesn't scream. She just takes it while she can.

Sidney Crybaby Bridge
(Shelby County)

A Bridge of Whispers

They call it the Sidney Crybaby Bridge—a simple metal-and-concrete overpass spanning a shallow creek near what was once the junction of Children's Home Road and South Main Avenue. To visitors, it looks perfectly ordinary. But by midnight, under a hissing moon, it becomes something else entirely.

Locals say: drive across the bridge after dark... and listen.

Who Fell, Who Was Pushed

No one knows for sure. Some maintain a baby slipped from a mother's arms. Others say she was thrown—along with her mother—into the currents below.

Over time, six different versions of her death took shape, but they all end the same:

Her final sound was a wail—a tortured, endless cry that could freeze the blood.

When the Midnight Tolling Starts

If you stop your car in the bridge's center and kill the engine, silence sets in. Too soon, too painfully—you'll hear it: A thin baby cry, echoing off the guardrails.

Occasionally, a piercing mother's scream follows.

Some say there's no wind—but the air feels like someone is sobbing nearby.

One driver said his headlights dimmed, and when he turned them back on, he saw…a small shape at the edge of the bridge—before it vanished into mist.

Why the Legend Persists

There's no police report. No coroner's file. No grave marker. Just the sound—a ghost story passed around campfires, shared by the River Road crowd, and whispered in suburban yards.

The story thrives because the bridge feels haunted.

At night, your car's radio might scratch or cut out here.

Your engine might stall—every time.

And if you leave without looking back, sometimes… you swear the cry follows you down the road.

The Haunting of Fulton Lock 4
(Stark County)

Long ago, when the canals still mattered, a furious lock tender at Fulton Lock 4 snapped.

Learning the lock would be shut for good, he went mad—dousing his fellow workers with acid and sealing the cabin. Their skin sloughed off over days of agony. Then, he turned the acid on himself. They all died screaming. Now, at night, the air around Lock 4 pulses with groans and wet, gurgling cries.

The Headless Ghost of Bailey Bridge
(Summit County)

A Stranger, a Storm, and a Killing

On the night of April 13, 1853, a storm churned over Cuyahoga Falls. In its shadow walked two Englishmen—William Beatson, a butcher with questionable riches, and James Parks, a grave robber, poacher, and man with murder in his past. They never made it to Pittsburgh. Instead, the men drank their way across Hudson and wound up at Hall's Tavern in the Falls.

Rain pelted the wooden streets. By midnight, they were thrown out into the storm. One man would vanish. The other would be found headless.

Blood on the Bridge

At dawn, boys discovered bloody rags and a cane beneath the old Gaylord's Grove Bridge. A strip of cloth. A cracked bottle. Bits of brain clinging to the stones.

Beatson's body was found floating naked in the Cuyahoga River. His skull had been hacked clean off—never recovered. Parks fled but was captured, convicted, and hanged in 1854. But it didn't end there.

The Ghost Who Won't Rest

Sam, a local man, once confided in historian Gilbert Roberts that he had seen something while crossing the Bailey Bridge late one night. He'd been drinking. Maybe that explained it.

But the train lights caught a figure—a long coat. No head. Leaning over the edge of the bridge like he was searching the waters below—for something missing.

Others have seen him, too. Always on rainy nights. Always when it's too late to turn back.

The Curse of the Missing Head

They say Beatson can't move on. Until his head is found and laid to rest with his body, his ghost will remain. Searching. Watching. Waiting.

The Ghostly Aftermath of the Murder of Frances Maria Buel

(Trumbull County)

A Daughter's Life Taken

In the blistering summer of 1832, sixteen-year-old Frances Maria "Maria" Buel lived under the weight of a broken home. When her stepfather, Ira W. Gardner, murdered her in cold blood—stabbed her twice in the chest and stomach—it shook all of Trumbull County. He lured Maria away from safety, struck her, and confessed.

Sentenced to death, Gardner became the only man ever publicly hanged in Trumbull County, his grim fate carried out on November 1, 1833.

A Grave That Never Sleeps

In East Gustavus Cemetery, under the shade of a slender maple, lies Maria's headstone: plain, fragile, and often chilled by unseen sorrow. The marker bears her name and murder date—August 8, 1832. Over time, it cracked and was replaced, yet the grief anchored in that plot never faded.

Phantoms of Betrayal

At dusk, visitors have reported seeing:

- A pale young woman in white, drifting near Maria's grave
- Frozen tears glistening on her cheeks
- Mournful humming or lullabies, soft enough to freeze the blood
- Flickering lights and dead cameras, when pointed at her headstone

Some say she's still searching—for justice. Flowers left at her grave often wilt by dawn as though some lingering hand has tipped them toward death.

Final Word

Arrive just before dusk, slip among the stones, and you might catch her eyes—a sorrowful gaze that reaches right through you.

But listen close, and you'll hear it: a soft weeping, the echo of betrayal.

The Sugar Creek Wraith
(Tuscarawas County)

In the early morning hush of June 1880, John Krause trudged barefoot into Sugar Creek after spotting what looked like a bloated, burlap sack drifting beneath the Shanesville Road bridge. The waters were calm. The shape bobbed gently—too large for trash, too still for anything alive. When he reached it, he found the fabric swollen and tightly tied, with something hard and lumpy within. Krause recoiled. He let the current take it. But he couldn't shake the image.

The Dreaded Unwrapping

That evening, Krause returned with other coal miners, among them William Deiser. They dragged the sack from the creek while curious townsfolk formed a silent ring. As the knots were loosened, a stench rushed up like breath from the dead—a rotting, sickly-sweet reek that sent hands flying to mouths. The sack fell open with a sucking noise. Inside: blackened flesh, a calico dress soaked dark, walnut shells, a brick, and near the center—a head twisted awkwardly into the folds of cloth. The skin sloughed, the jaw hung askew. The body had been burned, broken, and then dumped like refuse.

Mary Senef's Fate

Eighteen-year-old Mary Senef had been missing for weeks. She had worked as a house servant for the Crites and Athey families on Stone Creek, helping Ellen Athey recover from a miscarriage. Her sister Sarah had grown suspicious when she received a letter, clumsily written, claiming Mary had left for Indiana. The handwriting was wrong. And Mary never left without saying goodbye.

Ash and Bone

Authorities visited the Crites farm on June 16. The smell hit them first. Behind the house, a blackened heap of ashes reeked of blood and rot. When they dug into it, they unearthed scraps of calico, burnt cabbage, walnut shells, and what looked like scorched flesh. The barn wagon nearby was slick with mud and wet ash. Inside the home, a pair of charred shoe buttons lay in the stove. And an ax—its edge still dark—rested in the wagon, soaked in coal dust and dried blood.

A Murder Born of Madness

Ellen Athey confessed. Her voice was flat. Her words almost proud. She had murdered Mary in a jealous fury, wrongly believing the girl seduced her husband. *The young girl had not.* Ellen claimed the rage had begun with a dream and festered into something monstrous. One morning, while Mary worked unaware, Ellen struck her with an ax. Then buried the body. But it wouldn't stay buried.

The smell clawed through the dirt. So, she summoned her husband and brothers to help. They dug Mary up, stuffed her in cloth, weighed her with bricks, and hurled her into Sugar Creek like offal.

Ellen was sentenced. The others—Henry Athey, Alexander and Frank Crites—were eventually released. Only Ellen stood trial. But no court could settle what came next.

She Walks From the Water

Soon after, whispers spread—of something unnatural near the bridge. Mist that rose from the creek and took shape. Of a girl's form dripping and pale, walking the bridge rails with arms outstretched. Some saw her approach the houses, staring up at the windows with hollow, weeping eyes. Others heard a voice—low, raspy, and soaked with sorrow—calling out through the fog.

Mary never left Sugar Creek.

She was thrown away like garbage.

Now, she comes back.

The Haunted Union County Courthouse
(Union County)

The Union County Courthouse, built in 1841, stands as a historical landmark in Marysville. Over the years, it has become a focal point for local legends and ghost stories. Witnesses have heard unexplained noises and seen shadowy figures wandering its halls.

Dead Man Walking: Haunting of Woodland Cemetery

(Van Wert County)

The Warning Ignored

On a warm June evening in the 1880s, a Methodist minister made his way along Willshire Road in Van Wert, visiting relatives.

He had spent hours sipping lemonade, laughing, and chatting on the front porch as the sun set, only to realize that the roads would soon be swallowed by darkness.

His hosts urged him to stay, warning him about the dangers of wandering after dark—especially with reports of a strange, malevolent shadow near Woodland Cemetery. But the minister, scoffing at the idea of ghosts, brushed off their concerns. He laughed and insisted it was nothing but local superstition.

"Ghosts? Nonsense!" he chuckled, waving off their warnings with a confident, dismissive wave of his hand. He knew the cemetery well—it was newly established, with a mixture of new and old graves, and there was no reason to fear a place like that.

The Curse of Woodland Cemetery

The night air grew heavier as the minister left, the scent of fresh grass and the chirping of crickets filling the air. The road seemed endless, but his confidence kept him at ease—until he neared the cemetery.

As he approached, an unnatural chill wrapped around him, sending a sudden, suffocating dread through his chest. Tall evergreens stretched their limbs across the moonlit path, casting long, unnatural shadows that seemed to move of their own accord. The trees appeared to whisper, but it wasn't the wind that carried the sound—it was something else.

His feet grew heavy. The road ahead felt far longer than it was as if some invisible force was holding him back. Something wasn't right. As he stepped closer to the cemetery gates, a strange sensation of being watched washed over him.

He felt the cold breath of an unseen presence creeping up his spine.

Then, from the darkest corner of the cemetery, he saw it—a tall, black cadaver rising from the ground.

The Corpse That Walked

The figure was dressed in a ragged burial gown, and as it stood, it seemed to claw its way out of the earth, its fingers gnarled and bent. The eyes were hollow—dark voids in its skull, and the lips peeled away from its jagged teeth, revealing rows of rotten, broken teeth, more like fangs than anything human. Its movements were slow and deliberate, like a predator searching for prey.

As the minister stood frozen, his breath caught in his chest, the ghostly figure turned its head toward him. The eyes locked onto him, and they began to shuffle toward him with eerie, unnatural steps.

Frozen in terror, the minister found himself rooted to the spot, unable to move. His heart pounded in his chest as the corpse drew closer, its feet dragging across the earth. Finally, panic set in. He broke into a sprint, desperate to outrun the dead.

The Pursuit

The minister's feet pounded against the dirt road as he ran, but he could hear the shuffling of the ghost's feet close behind. With every breath, the terror deepened. He knew he had to distance himself. But as he neared a secluded spot near the road, he realized something—they were going to meet at the same point.

Desperate to stay ahead, he slowed his pace, trying to keep a distance of about 20 feet between them. The ghost moved with slow, methodical steps, utterly unaware of the minister's careful maneuvering.

Just when the minister thought he might escape, the ghost turned abruptly into the brushy area, its form disappearing into the dark. The minister's heart raced, but as he passed by, he looked desperately for the figure; there was no sign of it. No movement, no shadows—just empty space where the dead man had vanished.

The Unmarked Grave

As the minister continued walking, he stumbled upon something that stopped him dead in his tracks. Hidden in the overgrown thicket, nearly lost to time, was a neglected grave, its headstone worn and partially buried beneath the surrounding vegetation. A sense of dread filled his chest as he realized the truth. This grave, forgotten by most, had once been the final resting place of the man who had risen from the dead. The townspeople, thinking they were doing a good deed, had moved the body to Woodland Cemetery. But the spirit of the man had never agreed with this, and it would not rest until it returned to the land it called home. The minister finally understood. The grave had been disturbed—and the ghost would never stop searching until it was returned to its rightful place.

Final Word

The ghost of the man still walks near the cemetery, searching for the grave that was taken from him, seeking vengeance on those who disturbed his eternal rest. If you ever find yourself near Woodland Cemetery at night, and you feel the presence of something behind you—don't look back. Don't call out. Because once you see those hollow eyes, you might never leave the woods.

Moonville Brakeman: "That's Mine."
(Vinton County)

A Tunnel, a Town, and a Trail of Ghosts

The town of Moonville is long gone. All that remains is a lonely stretch of abandoned track swallowed by the woods, a crumbling tunnel carved through rock, and whispers that follow hikers when the wind dies. Once, during the coal boom of the 19th century, trains thundered through here. The work was brutal. The air was thick with smoke.

Men clung to the sides of railcars with raw hands and frozen breath. And above it all, on the roofs of moving trains, walked the brakemen.

The Job That Took Men Apart

In those early days of the railroad, trains didn't slow easily. Brakemen were the ones who did the work—climbing up ladders, leaping between cars in motion, and turning rusted wheels in driving rain, snow, or wind.

It was dangerous.

Men lost their footing and fell between the cars.

Others were decapitated when they failed to duck in time beneath tunnels like the one at Moonville.

They worked drunk.

They worked dead tired.

And some didn't live long enough to learn from their mistakes.

The Man Who Slept on the Rails

One brakeman, known only to the drink and the tracks, stumbled along the line between Zaleski and Moonville one damp night.

He clutched a bottle of whiskey like it was a compass.

With every step, he drank.

With every sip, he sagged.

The forest breathed around him—wet, black, and quiet. The tunnel loomed ahead. But he didn't make it.

He laid down instead. Rails for a pillow. Track for a bed.

And sometime before the sun rose, a train roared through the dark and took off his head.

His skull bounced down into the ravine below, lost to the flood-swollen waters of a creek. His body landed neatly in the brush, legs crossed like he'd gone peacefully. The bottle, miraculously intact, spun once in the center of the rails and came to rest without spilling more than a drop.

The Voice That Warned

At dawn, with rain still falling, a miner walking to the Zaleski mines spotted the bottle glinting between the rails. He bent down to claim the prize.

Just as his fingers touched the glass, a voice scraped out from the fog: "That's mine."

The miner froze. He looked left. Right. No one.

Then, blood. Small, dark specks on the stones.

He followed the trail over the rail bed and into the thicket where the ballast gave way to brush—and parted the leaves with trembling hands. There, curled neatly between root and stone, was the headless body of the brakeman. Still clutching nothing.

The Head That Was Never Found

The miner fled, screaming back to Moonville as thunder cracked overhead. A party returned with shovels and lanterns. They buried the body beside the tracks. But they never found the head. Searchers combed the ravine. They waded the creek even as it spilled over its banks in the storm.

But the brakeman's skull was gone—swept into the earth or stolen by something older than the rails.

The bottle remained. And that... became the problem.

The Bottle No One Can Keep

The whiskey bottle sat in the same place on the tracks for years. Occasionally, someone would try to pick it up.

The voice would come each time just as their hand brushed the glass. Raspy. Angry. Closer than it should be: "That's mine."

Fingers would recoil. Faces would drain pale.

Some dropped the bottle and ran.

Others claimed they felt a cold hand grip their wrist—something headless, something blind, but not lost.

No one kept the bottle for long. But still, it sits there.

Waiting.

Walk Softly Past the Tunnel

Today, hikers walk the old Moonville rail trail, crossing the bridge and passing through the tunnel, never knowing what sleeps just beneath the ballast stones.

Some say if you stop near the tracks at dusk, you'll see the glint of a bottle.

Some say if you bend to touch it, you'll hear the gravel shift behind you.

And some say, if you listen long enough, you'll hear a voice—low, wet, and broken—call out from the dark with finality: "That's mine."

The Hatchet Murders of Waynesville
(Warren County)

It was the stench that gave them away.

For nearly three days in the suffocating heat of late August 1879, no one had entered or left the small whitewashed cottage on South Main Street in the quiet Quaker town of Waynesville. The blinds stayed drawn. The windows shut tight. Neighbors spoke of screams that had pierced the night like a knife—but no one checked. Not until the house began to rot from within.

A Door Forced Open, and Hell Behind It

When a local constable and a retired judge forced the swollen door open, the air that spilled out was thick with death. Inside, the parlor had become a charnel room.

Laid out in a grotesque tableau were the butchered bodies of Mollie Hatte, age 37; her sister Clementine Weeks; and Clementine's 11-year-old daughter, Myrtle—all hacked to pieces with a hatchet.

One corpse—Myrtle's—had been there the longest. Her face was chewed and hollowed by rats, her limbs at crooked, unnatural angles.

Clementine's arms had been raised in final defense, nearly severed at the elbows.

Mollie lay slumped near the fireplace, her head caved in, the handle of the murder weapon—splintered and slick with blood—discarded nearby like firewood.

A Son Vanishes, Then Hangs

The only other resident of the house, Mollie's 18-year-old son Willie Anderson, was nowhere to be found.

Within days, his body was discovered—hanged in a barn, his face bloated, tongue blackened and protruding.

Whether he had witnessed the murders, helped commit them, or was simply unable to live with what had happened, no one ever knew.

He left no note.

No confession. Only more questions. The murders were never solved.

No solid motive ever surfaced.

No justice was served.

The Haunting Never Stopped

Eventually, the cursed house was torn down, plank by bloody plank. But the land remained tainted.

Locals reported strange lights flickering near the road, and some swore they saw a young girl in a tattered dress walking along the edge of the property, barefoot and bleeding, her face pale and mouth open in a silent scream.

They say it's Myrtle, still searching for her mother... still wandering the place where she died.

And if you walk South Main alone at night, you might hear the whisper of a child.

Or the wet thud of a hatchet.

The Haunted Hollow of Kings Mills
(Warren County)

Deep in the woods along the Loveland Bike Trail, where moss clings to crumbling brick, riders report twisted, shadowy figures darting across the path. Faces stare from shattered windows. A baby cries—sharp, sudden—then silence. In 1890, a train slammed into two cars loaded with 800 kegs of gunpowder. The blast ignited another 800.

Twelve died. One was a baby. Some say she still cries.

Floating Eliza
(Washington County)

It took ten years to build—and nearly no time at all for it to become a house of death.

In the 1850s, Douglas Putnam poured $65,000 into a lavish Italianate villa carved from the sandstone hills of Marietta, Ohio. It was meant to be a dream for his wife, Eliza—a copy of a grand New Jersey mansion she'd adored. Twenty-two rooms. Tower. Widow's walk. A view of the Ohio and Muskingum rivers.

Eliza wanted opulence. She got a tomb.

Just three years after the final stone was set, Eliza dropped dead from heart disease. She never really moved in. And something never moved out.

After Douglas's death and years of passing hands, the Anchorage became a nursing home. That's when the shadows started.

Stairway Specter

Patients whispered of a woman on the stairs— floating, pale, silent. A nurse saw her gliding toward the dining room, her feet never touching the ground. Another aide saw a flickering light twist and dance across the widow's walk—though no one was around.

The Woman on the Lawn

One couple, stopping for a daytime tour, never even made it inside. The woman froze at the car—her voice gone. Just beyond the yard, a figure hovered in the midday air. A full-bodied ghost, inches above the grass. Eliza, they say. Still waiting. Still watching. A bag in her hand as if she wished to take all her lavishness with her.

Eliza's Curse

Now, strange voices echo through empty rooms. Guests report icy hands tugging their hair. Passersby glimpse a face staring back from the upstairs windows— though the house is locked tight.

The Ghost Train of the River Styx
(Wayne County)

Rittman, Ohio – March 22, 1899

It was just past dawn when Erie westbound Passenger Train No. 5 barreled toward Sterling, thundering along at 60 miles per hour. The air was cold, wet, and silent—until it wasn't. As the engine roared across the trestle spanning a narrow waterway named with uncanny dread—the River Styx—it buckled. A sickening groan of metal filled the hollow. Then the train jumped the tracks.

The cars crumpled like paper. All but the dining car tumbled, snapping beams, tearing limbs, pulverizing bone. Engineer Alexander Logan, 48, never saw it coming. The engine rolled, crushing him beneath tons of screeching steel. When rescue crews pulled his body free, they found his spine broken, skull split, one eye open— staring mindlessly at the river below.

A Return to the Dead

Seven months later, a local doctor and his companion were returning from a house call when they paused along the tracks. The rails began to tremble. A train approached. Just as it reached the Styx trestle, the whistle screamed—long and humanlike. The engine slammed into reverse, belching smoke and catching fire.

The crash tore through the night.

They watched in frozen horror as cars twisted in the air, steam roared like an animal, and screams erupted from inside splintered wreckage. But when they ran to help, the wreck was gone. So was the fire. The tracks lay empty and clean. No train had passed.

Whispers from the River

Over the next year, more townsfolk saw it. Some heard shrieks at dawn. Others saw phantom cars hurtle into the ravine—only to vanish. By 1901, the legend had choked the town. Locals called it an omen. But no new tragedy followed.

Still, the trestle stands. The River Styx still runs beneath it. And on the blackest, stillest nights, the ghost of Train No. 5 howls down the tracks once more. Screams echo in the hollows. Flames light up the trees.

A shadowed figure—Logan, perhaps—can sometimes be seen beneath the bridge, dragging what's left of his shattered body toward the water's edge.

Some say he never made it out.

And the train is still trying.

Fortress for the Damned
(Williams County)

Built in 1869, the Williams County Jail in Bryan rose like a stone box for the condemned. Its thick Romanesque walls—cut from rough, local masonry—housed the lowest of society: thieves, murderers, drunks, and madmen. Inside, rusted iron bars confined them to narrow upper-floor cells, where light seldom reached and heat withered in the winter.

Men hanged themselves from the pipes or starved quietly, refusing to eat in protest or despair.

At least two executions took place here—officially. The rest left pieces of themselves behind.

Although the jail shut down in the late 20th century and was restored brick by brick, those who enter say it still has a presence. It hums with the tension of things unfinished. Of judgment still echoing off the walls.

Things That Watch in the Dark

- In the far corridor near solitary confinement, multiple guests and investigators have seen the same figure: a tall man in 19th-century deputy's clothing, pacing like he's still on duty. He doesn't respond. He doesn't stop.

- Cell 3 is colder than the rest. People report crushing sadness, like something grieving inside the brick. One psychic wept upon crossing the threshold. In 2016, a paranormal group captured an EVP—a hoarse whisper rasping: "I was judged." The voice had no echo. The cell was empty.

- Downstairs in the processing room, a woman screamed when she saw a man curled beneath a desk, trembling like prey. When she called out, he vanished. His impression stayed in the dust.

The Hanging Never Stops

The gallows are long gone, but the sounds remain:

Footsteps overhead where there's no second floor. A metal door slams when no one is near it. The soft creak of a rope swaying just out of sight.

Visitors walking through the east wing often stop and clutch their throats.

A few have left gasping, insisting they felt something tighten around their necks, just for a moment. The air there is colder. Heavier.

The Sheriff Who Wouldn't Leave

Local lore recounts a sheriff who served into the 1890s, presiding over trials and executions with a heavy heart. He died at his desk, struck down by his own heart after witnessing one hanging too many. But they say he never really left.

Paranormal teams have captured his hat and boots in photographs—clear, sharp, and standing where no one stood. Visitors describe a presence behind them as if being followed just out of view. Always just behind the shoulder. Always watching.

The Weight of What Remains

What lingers in the old jail isn't playful. It doesn't move chairs or flicker lights for amusement. What's trapped here is solemn. Heavy. Residual pain locked behind mortar and steel.

Those who've walked the halls speak of one certainty:

It doesn't want to be forgotten. And it won't let you leave unchanged.

Drumming Dead of Nettle Lake
(Williams County)

Nettle Lake lies in Ohio's far northwest corner. Its stagnant waters touch close to the Michigan line. Shallow, overgrown, and known for sudden bursts of fog, the lake was once a remote and uneasy place—used by Native American tribes. It was later settled by frontiersmen who spoke of strange lights and animal remains left along the banks. It was never a lake that people swam in for long. Locals always said the ground beneath it was unsettled.

The Man Who Wanted Answers

In the late 1800s, Sam Coon, a wiry, half-crazed man from nearby Bridgewater Township, came to believe he could communicate with the dead. Not just any dead—but ancient Indian spirits. Sam was obsessed with rumors of buried tribal treasure beneath the swampy land around the lake.

He said the drumming could guide him.

He carved a drum from old wood and stretched deer hide across the top. At night, he would walk alone to the lake's edge, light a fire of willow bark and pine sap, and begin to beat the drum in slow, deliberate rhythms.

Thump.

Thump.

Thump.

People said they could hear it from miles away, even when the wind blew in the opposite direction.

The Last Summoning

In late October, Sam told the postmaster he'd found something. A spot near the north shore where the ground "shivered."

That night, he was seen walking down the Nettle Lake path with his drum and shovel.

He never came back.

Three days later, a dog brought home a piece of cloth soaked in blood.

A search party found Sam's campsite, but no body—only his drum, split in two and still damp.

One man claimed the fire pit was full of teeth.

The Curse Begins

Since then, people say Sam Coon still drums, especially before lightning storms or in the stillness before dawn. The beat comes slow at first, then quickens, as if something is being summoned from beneath the muck.

Some campers claim to see a man walking the lake's edge with no face, just dark hollow bone where eyes and mouth should be.

Others have reported hearing footsteps in the water, even when the surface lies flat.

Final Warning

If you walk Nettle Lake alone, and the wind dies down, listen.

If you hear the sound of a single drumbeat, do not answer it.

Do not follow it.

Sam Coon never found what he was looking for.

But something may have found him.

And now it drums to bring others to the same, soggy grave.

Ghoul Grave-eater
(Wood County)

In January 1884, a ghoul tore through Wood County, disturbing graves and causing chaos in cemeteries.

"It was no earthly creature." That's what the man said—his face pale, his hand still trembling. He'd seen it cross the frozen road near Fostoria on a bitter January night in 1884. The moonlight caught the white on its chest like a slash of bone, but the rest of it—black as rotten soil. It was long, low, and hunched. A thing that moved wrong... sluggishly, awkwardly.

Its tracks were worse. Wide claw marks, sharper than a man's knife, gouged into the snow. Eight inches long in the front, three wide. The back prints were almost round—like a dog if a dog clawed through pine boxes to get at the meat.

They say it burrowed through the frozen ground at the Perry Township graveyard. Dug deep. Dug fast. One grave at a time.

"It opens coffins," another man whispered. "It eats what's inside."

No bullet touched it. No blade bit it. One farmer swore it tore straight through his rail fence, leaving nothing but splinters. His dog—usually bold—chased it only a few paces before it came whining back, tail tucked, ribs heaving as if it had looked into hell itself.

"There was something about its head," the man said. "Too long. Too flat. And it never blinked."

At night, neighbors heard it—the horrible, wet crunch of it feeding. The sharp bark it gave when disturbed. A sound like a sob strangled in fury. And always, afterward, silence. Not even birdsong. "It travels with such rapidity that all attempts thus far to kill it have proved futile."

Next, it moved north. Toward Toledo. Toward more graves. And every time someone tried to stop it, all that was left behind... was open earth, clawed wood, and something half-eaten.

Until it just disappeared. Or did it?

Soul Saving Soul: Ghost at Dunbridge Oil Field
(Wood County)

In the late 1800s, a boiler exploded on the Roller family's Dunbridge Oil Field outside Bowling Green, ripping C.C. Clark and two men apart in a spray of steam, metal, and flesh. Their remains were scraped off the wreckage. Work resumed. Then, during a vicious storm, a lone pumper watched in horror as a charred figure sprinted from the shadows—its face blistered and bone-white, wrench clutched tight.

It leapt to the boiler and vanished—no footfalls, no sound—just the hiss of steam and the stink of lightning-charred air. The pumper stood paralyzed, heart pounding like a piston.

Slowly, he crept through the mud and rain toward where the figure had disappeared.

There, gleaming wet in the flicker of lightning, was a heavy iron wrench—resting dead center on the blow-off valve, just as Clark had held it the night he died.

But this time, nobody died.

The wraith had saved the pumper's life.

With shaking hands, the pumper shut the valve.

He lived. But he left that night, pale as a corpse, eyes wide and empty.

And after word spread, no one dared work the boiler again. Not one.

Skeleton in the Wall:
Woodbury House
(Wood County)

A House in the Wild

Before roads were roads and Bowling Green was little more than stumps and silence, the Woodbury family homestead stood alone in the thick, swamp-dark forests of Wood County. Built in the early 1800s, it was a modest house—two rooms, rough-hewn beams, a stone hearth— just enough to keep out the wolves and cold. But something else had found its way in.

A Night Visitor

Two hunters lost and trailing dusk, knocked on the door. They were let in, fed, and offered space by the fire. The night deepened. The wind scratched the shutters. One of the men awoke. Not to a noise—but to a rattling.

There was a slow, dragging sound across the floorboards. There, in the faint orange glow of dying coals, stood a figure—a man stripped to the bone, skull twisted, jaw slack, eyes hollow as the grave. He didn't speak. He raised one bony hand. And pointed to the wall. Then, it vanished into nothing.

The Bones Behind the Boards

Shaken, the hunter roused his companion. They told the Woodburys what had happened. Laughing nervously, someone fetched a prybar. The boards came off slowly, the wood groaning as if it remembered.

Inside, a human skeleton slumped between the studs. The jaw was broken. The skull was fractured. Some claimed the man had been a traveler, murdered for his coin. Others said he was buried there alive—screaming, unheard, as the wall was sealed.

It Did Not End There

Even after the bones were buried, the house underwent a change. Lights flared and died without cause. Cold spots bled through the walls like an infection.

Some swore they saw the skeleton return—dragging itself through the parlor, raising its hand, again and again, pointing to the place of its betrayal.

And long after the house fell to ruin, old-timers warned: It just waits. In the soil.

Ghostly Flames of Colonel William Crawford
(Wyandot County)

The Massacre Before the Fire

The Sandusky plains ran red before the fire ever came.

In March 1782, nearly a hundred peaceful Christian Lenape were butchered at Gnadenhutten by American militiamen—scalped, clubbed, and axed in cold blood, many while kneeling in prayer. The slaughter was total, the revenge inevitable.

Three months later, Colonel William Crawford marched through the tall grass along the Sandusky River, leading five hundred volunteers to attack nearby Native villages. He wanted a swift victory.

What he got was justice soaked in flame.

Death at Tymochtee Creek

They were waiting for him—440 Delaware warriors and British allies—silent, precise, and prepared. The clash was brief. Crawford's expedition unraveled like a wet cloth. Dozens were killed. Dozens more were captured. Crawford was among them.

And when word spread that some of his men had butchered innocents at Gnadenhutten, the deliberation ended. Crawford was dragged to a post near Tymochtee Creek, stripped and bound. And the fire began.

Two Hours in Hell

They cut off his ears. They scalped him, still alive. They heaped hot embers and coals at his feet, forcing him to dance as his flesh cooked. They stabbed him repeatedly, only to keep him conscious.

For two hours, the colonel screamed until his voice turned to a hoarse gargle. When he collapsed, they shoveled coals onto his chest. When he gasped again, they thrust burning sticks into his mouth. By the end, he was more ash than man.

The Haunting Along the Creek

Settlers came decades later, and with them came stories. Near the banks of Tymochtee Creek, on nights when the wind was still, a figure was seen.

It hovered above the soil—limbs smoldering, eyes hollow, and a ring of flame curling around its body. Some said it tried to speak but could only emit a wet, bubbling hiss, as though lungs still boiled inside a scorched chest.

Dogs refused to approach the spot.

Even now, near High Bank or close to Ritchy Cemetery, the apparition returns—wandering through flickering firelight, trapped in his final agony.

He burns still. Not for glory. Not for honor.

But for what was done.

My Ghost Story
(Vinton County)

People often ask me if I believe in ghosts. I do, but I approach the topic with a healthy dose of skepticism. They usually follow up with, "Alright, so has anything ever happened to you?" The answer is yes. I have visited thousands of haunted places while researching my books, which increases the likelihood that I've had more than a few strange and ghostly experiences. Here is one of my favorites from the haunted Moonville Tunnel area.

They say the dead don't walk the Moonville Rail Trail.

They stalk. They slither. They crawl. And, apparently... they purr.

I've hiked that trail for years. I've seen and heard things I couldn't explain. Still, nothing unsettled me more than the thing that started following me from King Hollow—something small, light-footed, and deceptively sweet.

A cat. Or something that used to be.

The Meowing in the Brush

It started like any other stray encounter. I was hiking near the cut by the old King Hollow station when I heard it—that unmistakable feline wail. That miserable, long, dragging *Meeeooowww* from deep in the brush. A cry too sad to ignore. It echoed like a plea across the rail bed.

I followed the sound. Through bramble.

Through blood-hungry thorns.

Through the kind of underbrush that leaves scars that you don't brag about. Each time, the cry moved just ahead—tugging me deeper, always just out of reach.

A glimpse here. A flicker of fur there. Then nothing.

And yet, on the path again, it would come padding up behind me, weaving through my legs like it wanted to trip me. Typical cat behavior. Pet me or perish. Then it vanished as if the air itself swallowed it up.

The Dog That Didn't Bark

Now, I should've known something was off when Harley didn't react. Harley is my rescue mutt, trail companion, and certified cat-hater. I've seen her stiffen like a board at the faintest whiff of feline.

She doesn't chase—oh no. Harley prefers psychological warfare. She'll lift one lip like a snide threat, show a single glint of canine ivory, and growl so low it sounds like the dirt's doing the talking.

If a cat even thinks about crossing our path, Harley knows. But not this one.

When the ghost cat first started following us, Harley didn't growl. She didn't snarl. She didn't even notice. Her hackles stayed flat. Her nose stayed dry. Not once did she so much as twitch. It was like the thing wasn't even there. Which, of course, it wasn't. Not exactly.

The Cat That Wasn't

Now, I believe in ghosts—but I like to rule out raccoons, possums, wind, and weird lighting before I start blaming the undead. So I kept trying to catch the cat. With hands. With food. With reason. But I was always a step too slow. Or it was a step too smart.

Then came the night I left my trail cam set up at Moonville Tunnel. I'd finished my hike and left it recording the mouth of the tunnel for about fifteen minutes while I packed up. There were no cat calls that night. No brushing against my leg. No meows.

But when I got home and played the video... there it was. A meow. Plain as daylight.

Crisp, clean, and close—like it came from just outside the frame. And no cat to be seen.

The Theory

I've come to believe that the little beast is a remnant. A spectral leftover. Someone's long-dead pet still patrolling the tracks of a town long buried by time and trees.

Maybe it's still looking for its owner. Perhaps it's playing. Or maybe it just likes watching hikers trip over their own feet in panic.

I should warn you, though: people who try to pet it sometimes have the little beast follow, wrapping around their ankles waiting to be fed.

So if you're walking the Moonville Rail Trail, and you hear a meow—don't go calling, "Here, kitty kitty."

Don't offer it treats. And for the love of God, don't try to pet it. Because if you do... it might follow you home.

Haunted Shorts

·Serpent Mound Shadows – Adams County

Ghostly shadows and an uncanny energy are said to hover above the prehistoric Serpent Mound at dusk.

·Adams County Jail White Figure – Adams County

An apparition in white robes has been seen drifting through the corridors of the old West Union jail at night.

·Still House Hollow Phantom – Fairfield County

A half-calf, half-man creature reportedly climbed onto a passing horse on Foglesong Road before disappearing into the darkness.

·Elmwood Cemetery Figures – Fairfield County

Witnesses describe a hooded figure, a little girl, and even a witch specter wandering the graves at night.

·Mathias Cabin Faces – Fairfield County

Ghostly faces peer from a lit cabin at night in Clear Creek Metro Park, as if still occupying the home.

·Ash Cave Pale Lady – Hocking County

A woman in 1920s style clothing appears walking the Ash Cave trail at dusk before disappearing into the woods.

·Concord Church Cemetery Lady – Athens County

At night, an elderly woman is seen rocking an empty cradle near the old church graveyard.

·Millfield Mine Disaster Spirit – Athens County

At the site where 82 men died in a 1930 mine explosion, the ground reportedly vibrates underfoot as if echoing their final moments.

·Faces of Athens Lunatic Asylum – Athens County

Ghostly faces, voices, and footsteps are often reported at the old Athens asylum.

•Luhrig Road Screamer – Athens County

A woman who died in a house explosion has been seen running along the road at night, her dress aflame.

•King Station Lady – Athens County

A pale apparition of a woman haunts the abandoned railroad tracks at King Station after slitting her throat in the 1870s.

•Elmore Rider – Sandusky County

Every spring a motorcyclist retraces his fatal ride over Muddy Creek.

•Dead Man Hollow – Scioto County

Phantom screams echo through Shawnee State Forest where a traveling peddler's body was found.

•White Lady Point – Scioto County

Boaters along the Ohio River have long seen a screaming woman atop a bluff near Portsmouth.

•Conkle's Hollow Figures – Hocking County

Shadows of condemned Native Americans are seen drifting among the sandstone cliffs and forested trails.

•Simcoe Ghost – Hocking County

A smoky apparition emits mournful cries along an isolated hollow near an abandoned shack.

•Rockhouse Hotel Mary – Hocking County

The spirit of young Mary is seen wandering the shelter area where the old Rockhouse Hotel once stood.

•Samuel Moore House Spirit – Pickaway County

The ghost of an escaped slave is said to linger at the historic Underground Railroad site near a rural farmhouse.

•Circleville Courthouse Soldier – Pickaway County

An apparition of a Union soldier walks the upper floors of the old courthouse after dark.

·Paul Peters Farm Shadow – Pickaway County

Shadow figures and blinking red lights haunt the cemetery where cholera victims were buried.

·Robinson's Cave Miners – Perry County

Ghostly miners who once protested for better working conditions are said to roam the cave at New Straitsville.

·Santoy Ghost Lady – Perry County

A translucent woman floats above the ground on the old town's deserted roadway.

·Roseville Prison Ghosts – Perry County

At the abandoned brick prison, ghostly faces appear in windows and on the grounds at night.

·Beech Grove Cemetery Bell Ghost – Perry County

You can hear a phantom church bell and see moving shadow forms at Beech Grove Cemetery.

·Vanishing Farmer of Scioto Trail – Ross County

A gaunt man stares down travelers before disappearing mysteriously into the roadside trees.

·Elizabeth's Grave – Pleasant Valley Cemetery – Ross County

The ghost of Elizabeth emerges as mist beneath a tree and returns if her marker is moved.

·Moonville Tunnel Apparitions – Vinton County

Ghosts of an engineer, brakeman, the Lavender Lady, and the Bully still linger in the foggy rail tunnel.

·Lake Hope Ghost Town Spirits – Vinton County

Trail-goers report a ghostly worker walking atop the ruins of the iron furnace stack carrying a lantern.

·Elevator Brewery Ghost – Franklin County

The spirit of a man killed in a winter altercation is seen walking the snow-covered yard after dark.

•Wooly Booger Cemetery– Franklin County

A Bigfoot like figure haunts the cemetery's trees near Big Darby Creek, often accompanied by flickering lights.

•Glen Echo Park Apparition – Franklin County

Visitors report the ghost of an old man who committed suicide roaming paths after sunset.

•Charles Breuer Eyes – Hamilton County

Visitors feel watched by the glass eyes set in the bust on his grave that seem to follow them.

•Ryan's Tavern Phantom – Butler County

Full-body apparitions have appeared seated at tavern tables as carts move on their own.

•Madison Seminary Haunting – Lake County

Formerly a Civil War-era hospital and institution, the building is now known for eerie locked-door apparitions and cold spots.

•Tiedemann House (Franklin Castle) – Cuyahoga County

This Victorian mansion is plagued by whispers, cold spots, and fleeting shadowy figures.

•Wolcott House Museum Hauntings – Lucas County

Playful household spirits move objects and open doors inside this historic museum home.

•Fallen Timbers Battlefield– Lucas County

Ghostly soldiers from the 1794 battle are said to appear at the battlefield site to spook passing motorists.

•Eden Park Gazebo Tragedy – Hamilton County

The spirit of Imogene wanders the Spring House Gazebo after being shot in a tragic incident there.

•Music Hall Ghosts – Hamilton County

Built over an old potter's field, the Music Hall holds rumors of restless spirits throughout its wings.

•Château Laroche (Loveland Castle) Apparitions – Hamilton County

Volunteers and visitors report odd noises and unexplained footsteps echoing through the medieval-style castle.

•Lafayette Hotel Spirit – Washington County

The ghost of Durwood Hoag has been seen on the third floor, along with chairs moving on their own.

•Stumpy's Hollow Headless Rider – Muskingum County

At the ravine behind the Norwich church, a headless specter known as Stumpy—believed to be the ghost of Christopher Baldwin—appears after dark.

•Woolen Mill Ghost – Wayne County

The spirit of a young man who fell into a mill wheel near Rogue's Hollow returns each evening to finish the work he never could complete.

•Crybaby Bridge Lament – Wayne County

At Rogues Hollow, the ghost of a mother eternally mourns her drowned infant, with wails echoing under the old bridge.

•Buckeye Belle Explosion Haunting – Washington County

On foggy fall nights at Beverly Lock, the echoes of a tragic riverboat explosion return as whistles and mournful voices

•Mound Cemetery Lights – Washington County

Strange lights drift atop the ancient earthen mound in Marietta's historic cemetery at twilight.

•Bowling Green Poorhouse Spirits – Wood County

The Wood County Historical Center is haunted by former residents from the old poorhouse.

•Nazareth Hall Hooded Figure – Wood County

A cloaked spirit walks the halls and grounds of Nazareth Hall in Grand Rapids.

·Holcomb Road School Bus Wreck Ghosts – Wood County

Ghostly children are seen near the site of an urban legend where a driver wrecked in the woods, killing its passengers.

· Scotts Creek Couple – Hocking County

The spirits of newlyweds Clara and Johannes replay their fatal creek crossing, along with phantom horse cries.

·Willoughby Cemetery Girl in Blue – Lake County

A mysterious Girl in Blue haunts the Willoughby Village Cemetery, often seen drifting among the headstones at dusk.

·Ghost of Mary Stockum's Grave – Coshocton County

At St. John's Lutheran Cemetery, the headless apparition of Mary Stockum was reportedly seen walking among the graves after nightfall.

·Dead Man's Curve Phantom – Clermont County

Ghostly forms of a man killed in a historic wreck appear walking the infamous curve and along the adjoining roadway.

·Lucy Run Cemetery Ghost – Clermont County

A spectral woman in a white gown runs from the stream up to the gates of Lucy Run Cemetery under moonlight.

·Crybaby Bridge Haunting – Lorain County

Visitors crossing the bridge in Vermilion hear a baby crying, and sometimes see tiny handprints mysteriously etched into nearby windows and doors afterward.

·Lonesome Lock Murderer Spirit – Summit County

Along the Ohio & Erie Canal at Lonesome Lock, a ghost of a murdered man walks the trail.

·Gypsy Grave Woman – Marion County

In St. Mary's Cemetery, the beloved local "Gypsy" who died during childbirth walks at night, with visitors leaving tokens at her grave.

·President Harding Apparition – Marion County

The spirit of President Warren G. Harding is rumored to linger at the Harding Home in Marion, occasionally seen in period attire.

·Twin City Opera House Ghost – Morgan County

At the old opera house in McConnelsville, a ghostly usher and the echo of women's voices are said to still appear during evening hours.

·Brownella Cottage Specter – Crawford County

People near the Brownella Cottage in Galion have seen the full-body apparition of Bishop Brown and heard unexplained footsteps echoing through the glass causeway.

·Ethyl's Sandusky River Ghost – Crawford County

The spirit of young Ethyl Hanley, killed in a carriage accident, is often seen walking the banks of the river where she once gathered flowers.

·Valentine Theatre Boy – Defiance County

A boy in period clothing reportedly appears inside the Valentine Theatre in Defiance, often seen standing near the stage in the dark.

·Schines Strand Lobby Man – Delaware County

The spirit of a man in vintage dress has been seen lingering in the lobby of the old Strand Theatre in Delaware, often late at night.

·Blue Limestone Park Lights – Delaware County

Near Delaware's Blue Limestone Park, glowing lights drift at the old train wreck site, tied to ghosts of crash victims.

·Abbot Tomb Pioneers – Erie County

The ghosts of Benjamin and Lorena Abbott—two early settlers—are rumored to haunt their namesake tomb in Milan Cemetery at dusk.

•Staley Road Strange Encounters – Clark County

Visitors on the rural Staley Road report unsettling sightings—dark figures along the road, odd sounds, and a heavy sense of dread under its canopied trees.

•Walhalla Ravine Mooney Mansion– Franklin County

Local lore in Clintonville tells of blue lights and spectral figures at Mooney Mansion, and ghostly reflections appearing under the nearby Calumet Street Bridge at night.

•Shades of Death Forest Figures – Gallia County

Between Cadmus and Patriot, there are reports of a hanged woman's ghost, phantom headlights, falling boulders, and shadowy humanoid shapes at dusk.

•Bellville Opera House Phantom – Richland County

A mischievous spirit, believed to be the courthouse's former patriarch, is said to appear on the third floor of this historic opera house when the building is unoccupied.

•Ohio State Reformatory (Mansfield) – Richland County

This imposing stone prison has reports of shadow figures, unexplained footsteps, and cold spots throughout its cells and hallways.

•Victoria Theatre Phantom – Montgomery County

When backstage dressing rooms are empty, some performers report hearing rustling of 19th-century taffeta and seeing the face of a vanished actress in mirrors—ghostly echoes of its vanished past.

• Blacks Cemetery near New Carlisle- Clark County

Visitors have reported hearing disembodied voices and seeing shadowy apparitions drifting among the tombstones.

•Amber Rose Restaurant Girl – Montgomery County

The apparition of Genevieve "Chickee" Ksiezopolski— is sometimes seen in an attic window.

·Bissman Building Entities – Richland County

At the historic warehouse, visitors report multiple hauntings—including a girl named Ruthie, a woman called Annabella, and a shadowy night watchman.

·Ye Olde Trail Tavern – Greene County County:

At this historic Yellow Springs tavern and former bakery, staff and visitors report the disembodied sobbing of a woman known as the "Woman in Blue." Some have even felt her brush past them upstairs.

·Ghost Girl at Dog Street Cemetery – Warren County

Within Kings Island's parking lot lies Dog Street Cemetery, where witnesses claim to see a little girl in a blue dress appear and dart in front of cars exiting the park—believed to be Missouri Jane Galeenor.

· John McAfee's Lantern Ghost – Montgomery County

The ghost of John McAfee, the first person convicted of a crime in Dayton (accused of poisoning his wife in 1801), wanders Third Street at night carrying a flickering lantern.

· Kalida Railroad Bridge Girl – Putnam County

At the old railroad bridge near Kalida, witnesses say a young girl's ghost walks along the tracks or beside the roadway, often disappearing when approached.

·Wild Woman of Coldwater – Mercer County

Legends from northern Mercer County speaks of a strange, disheveled woman seen roaming rural roads at night—known as the "Wild Woman of Coldwater"—who terrified area children and vanished as suddenly as she appeared.

· Pioneer Cemetery Whisperer – Trumbull County

In Warren's Mahoning Avenue Pioneer Cemetery, visitors recount hearing whispered words, lantern lights at dusk, and a gray cat that appears to follow lone ghost-walkers before vanishing.

·Woods School Headless Rider – Belmont County

At the abandoned Woods School property, a headless horseman asks passing travelers for saddlebags—said to be one of three men who vanished in 1845.

·Colonel Taylor Inn Haunting – Guernsey County

In Cambridge, the spirit of Colonel Taylor haunts the historic inn where he lived, with the faint aroma of pipe tobacco trailing through the stairwell and reports of creaking footsteps in his old bedroom, plus a mischievous ghost boy playing pranks.

·Palmer Road Crybaby Bridge – Mercer County

This infamous Mercer County bridge over the St. Mary's River is said to echo with the cries of a baby thrown off the bridge at night, and cars stalled when the engine is turned off—due to supernatural interference.

·Ghost Lights of Bessie / Melon Heads – Ottawa / Lake Counties

Though sometimes seen in Ottawa County, the most enduring legend is in Lake County (near Kirtland): strange "melon-head" creatures—shapeless humanoids with bulbous heads—are rumored to emerge from the oak forests near Wisner Road, often accompanied by unexplained lights in the trees.

·Milton Township Haunted Tunnel – Ashland County

Drivers who stop in the railroad tunnel on Twp Road 1536 claim that if they turn off their headlights and shift into neutral, unseen forces will push their car out the other side.

·Curtis Mansion Little Girl – Knox County

At the historic Curtis Mansion ("Round Hill") in Mount Vernon, a little girl is frequently seen peering from the second-floor windows, gazing down at passers-by in the evening hours.

- **Louiza Fox's Spirit – Belmont County** Though Belmont was covered earlier, including Louiza Fox fills a second unique county; the bereaved ghost of 13-year-old Louiza Catherine Fox is said to appear weeping near her grave in Salem Cemetery.

- **Beavercreek High School Teacher Ghost – Greene County**
The spirit of a murdered teacher is said to stalk the hallways and cafeteria of this former school, with footsteps and objects moving on their own, especially near the female staff areas.

- **Trail Tavern Lady in Blue – Greene County**
At Ye Olde Trail Tavern, visitors report seeing a smiling woman in a blue dress (believed to be Mary Hafner) roaming the upper floors, and sometimes another woman in black crying quietly upstairs.

- **Harvey Wells House Shadow – Jackson County**
In Wellston, the Harvey Wells House is haunted by its builder's ghost—his silhouette often appears at upper-floor windows, and staff report hearing footsteps after dark.

- **Big Green Castle Figures – Harrison County**
In the historic "Big Green Castle" residence, observers report shadowy figures in period clothing seen through second-story windows and mysterious lights moving inside.

- **ONU Ghost Brad – Hardin County**
At Ohio Northern University in Kenton, Presser Hall is haunted by "Brad," who knocks on pipes when music is played in D minor and sometimes swings a chandelier to the beat.

- **Deadman's Run Bridge Phantom – Richland County**
A spectral man is seen pacing across a rural bridge over Deadman's Run near Bellville, believed to be a drowned carriage driver.

·Headless Kate of Wildcat Hollow – Richland County

Tales from Wildcat Hollow speak of "Headless Kate," a beheaded woman haunting a little-used ravine road, searching endlessly for her lost head.

·Gold Mine Ghost – Richland County

On the road near Bellville, a doctor once stopped at night to investigate his horse's reluctance—and saw a blood-covered man standing beside a murdered body, then vanish before he moved.

·Big Black Dog Apparitions – Richland County

Near Zeiter's Cemetery north of Mansfield, witnesses over decades reported sightings of a giant black dog with glowing eyes—believed to manifest where an unmarked murder grave lies.

·Green Camp Haunted House – Marion County

Along old Green Camp Pike near Marion, there's a turn-of-century house believed to be haunted by witches and goblins—including reports that paranormal gatherings are held regularly on its grounds.

·Valley Steel Mill Moans – Clinton County

At the remnants of Valley Steel Mill in Clarksville, moans and screams are heard after dark—

·White Horse of Cuba – Clinton County

On cold, moonlit nights in the small town of Cuba, locals report seeing a ghostly white horse silently trotting lanes—leaving no tracks or sound yet disappearing before approached.

·Dug Hill Bridge Hunter – Auglaize County

A spectral hunter, shot and killed on Dug Hill Bridge once over the Auglaize River, chases startled travelers at night before vanishing into the woods.

•Meg's Grave Specter – Henry County (Crybaby Hill)

At Harris-Jones Cemetery (also known as Crybaby Hill) in McClure, mourners hear ghostly infant cries and occasionally see small phantom figures near old gravestones, some attributed to a tragic burial of infants.

•Punderson Manor Haunting – Geauga County

Guests at Punderson Manor, now a lodge in Punderson State Park, describe first-hand experiences with the ghost of its founder, Lemuel Punderson—often seen near the tower or corridors.

•Golden Lamb's Ghost Child – Warren County

Sarah Stubbs—or perhaps Eliza Clay, the daughter of Kentucky statesman Henry Clay—reportedly haunts the Golden Lamb Inn in Lebanon, with objects moving and laughter heard along the fourth-floor hallways.

•Fulton County Depot Girl – Fulton County

At the former Fulton Historical Museum—once a schoolhouse and hospital in Wauseon—staff describe a young boy staring from an upper window and a stern-dressed woman who appears in parlour areas, occasionally accompanied by objects being tossed or moved.